This Fragile Life

Other titles published by EPRINT Publishing:

A Death in the Family by Caroline Dunford
Missing Link by Elizabeth Kay
Spectacles by Pippa Goodhart
A Measure of the Soul by Stephanie Baudet

About the author:

David Webb was born and brought up in Anfield, Liverpool. Married with two children, he now lives in Bury where, before he became a full time writer at the turn of the new millennium, he worked as a primary school headteacher.

David is an established author of both children's fiction and resources for teachers, with over thirty titles to his name. His historical novels, including *Beneath the Bombers' Moon* and *Eye of the Storm*, have won critical acclaim. David travels the country providing talks and writing workshops in schools as well as delivering literacy courses and staff training sessions.

This Fragile Life is David's first novel for adults. The characters are drawn from keen observation and the plot is an enticing menu of humour, pathos and tragedy. In short, *This Fragile Life* is everybody's life.

This Fragile Life

David Webb

Published in Great Britain in 2009 by EPRINT Publishing
Blackburn, Lancashire
www.eprint.co.uk

© David Webb 2009

The moral right of David Webb as the author of this work has been asserted by him in accordance with the Copyright, Designs and Patents Act 1988.

This novel is a work of fiction. Names and characters are the product of the author's imagination and any resemblance to actual persons, living or dead, is entirely coincidental.

All rights reserved. No part of this publication may be reproduced, stored in a retrieval system, or transmitted, in any form or by any means, electronical, mechanical, photocopying, recording or otherwise, without the prior written permission of the copyright owner.

A CIP record for this work is available from the British Library.
ISBN 978-1-905637-87-4

Typeset in Great Britain by Educational Printing Services Limited, Blackburn, Lancashire
Printed and bound in Great Britain by CPI Cox & Wyman, Reading, Berkshire

Author's Note

This Fragile Life is the result of experience – not necessarily my personal experience but the experience of my journey through life so far. For all of us, the shadow of sudden change is ever present; a birth, a death, a broken relationship – events which can change and shape your life forever, sometimes for the better, sometimes for the worse. Look back into your past and you will surely find evidence of the fragility of life. Yet the story is optimistic because we are all resilient. Amidst the turmoil there is hope and humour and the promise of better times to come.

The main setting for my story is Didsbury in Manchester, a place where I spent three happy years as a student in the dim and distant past. You probably know people similar to some of the characters in the book; you will have met them in your own lives! I feel I should apologise to the present residents of Didsbury for altering the geography of the village. I hope you will understand that it was necessary in order to further the plot! A similar apology applies to the people of Whitby, the lovely Yorkshire coastal town which is also featured in the book.

Thank you for taking the time to read my story. I hope you enjoy your journey through *This Fragile Life*.

David Webb

For Glen, Jill and Stephen.

Chapter 1

'Mediocrity is the curse of the modern world.'

Matthew Hudson pulled up his zip and considered how this masterpiece of toilet wall graffiti summed up his life. He was twenty-nine years old and going nowhere. A job that bored him to bits and only just kept him financially viable; a terraced house in East Didsbury, damp and depressing, with a faulty central heating system and no discernible character; only one relationship of any meaning that had failed at the first hurdle five years ago.

Matt rinsed his hands under the cold water tap and pushed the stainless steel button on the automatic hand drier, glancing wistfully at the Durex machine. Nothing happened. He pushed the button again and then thumped the drier with his fist, cursing under his breath. He wiped his hands on his trousers and then pulled out his job card from an inside pocket. Three primary schools and a fitted kitchen shop – the same fitted kitchen shop he'd visited last week. What do they do to that computer? Still, he'd go in all smiles and politeness because that's what he was like. Good old friendly, reliable Matt with the permanent grin and the cheerful face. God – he hated his mediocre life.

There was never any room to park at primary schools. Matt drove through the narrow gates to be confronted by cars crammed into every available space. He sat for a moment and stared at them through the grey November drizzle, wondering whether to abandon his own vehicle where it was and collect it when the job was finished. A large blue delivery van pulled up behind him and, after waiting patiently for a whole three seconds, gave him a loud blast on the horn. Matt glared at the driver through his mirror and edged a little further forward before switching off his engine. He grabbed his black case from the passenger seat and got out of the car, glaring again at the van driver, who was sitting slumped over his steering wheel, chewing gum.

Matt walked down a few stone steps and followed a sign that directed visitors to the main entrance. St Gregory's Primary School. He had been there once before to install a system in the office. He remembered the Headmistress; a grey-haired woman in her late forties who looked permanently harassed and spoke in short, sharp sentences. The secretary had been all right, though. She had made him endless cups of strong coffee and had related the riveting experiences of her regular walking holidays in Snowdonia.

Matt pressed the security button and stood in the drizzle waiting for a response. After a few seconds, there was a crackling sound and a voice resembling a Dalek's rasped through the grill.

'Welcome to St Gregory's. How can I help you?'

'Matthew Hudson, from A1 Computer Systems.'

'Push the door when the buzzer sounds and come straight to the office to sign in, please.'

The buzzer sounded and Matt entered the building, stamping the drizzle from his shoes on a rubber mat just inside the doorway. There was the secretary, grinning at him through a glass panel built into a wall directly opposite the entrance. Matt grinned back and signed his name on a large visitor's pad.

'Nice to see you again,' said the secretary, sliding back the panel. 'Would you mind wearing a visitor's badge? Mrs Nelson will be with you in a minute.'

She looked as though she walked a lot. She had big thighs and Matt could picture her in waterproofs and a woolly hat.

Matt nodded and clipped the badge onto his jacket pocket. He was about to sit down on one of two charcoal grey chairs in the entrance area when the Headteacher's door opened and the grey-haired lady herself appeared.

'Sandra Nelson. Headmistress. Glad you could come so quickly.'

'No problem,' replied Matt, shaking her remarkably limp hand. 'I understand you've got a computer down? If you point me in the right direction I'll sort it out for you.'

'Year Three class,' snapped Mrs Nelson. She raised a hand and pointed. 'Along the corridor and second door left. It's happened before, you know. I'd like the job done properly this time.'

Matt nodded and grinned again and started off down the corridor. 'Get a life!' he muttered, as soon as he was out of earshot, and he glanced back like a naughty schoolboy.

There was a babble of voices coming from the classroom as Matt knocked on the green wooden door. He could see the children through the window, groups of maroon sweatshirts seated around rectangular tables, working away in lined exercise books, but there was no sign of a teacher. He knocked again and he entered, closing the door behind him. Two young boys on the nearest table glanced up at him and then got on with their work, ignoring him completely. Matt wasn't sure what to do. He approached one of the boys and tapped him on the arm.

'Is your teacher around? I'd like a word with her.'

The boy fixed Matt with a suspicious stare before turning to his friend and saying, 'George – he wants to speak to Miss.'

'Who are you?' asked George, chewing the end of his pencil. 'What are you here for?'

Matt felt really uncomfortable. He was being interrogated by a seven-year-old who ate pencils.

'Just tell me where your teacher is,' said Matt. His voice was firm but there was a definite irritation. 'I need to speak to your teacher.'

George's eyes narrowed. He stared at Matt for a few more seconds, scratched his mop of curly brown hair and then stood up and pointed across the room. Matt followed the line of his finger towards a group of children seated near the window, another cluster of rectangular tables surrounded by little maroon bodies. And then he noticed that one of the bodies wasn't maroon, it was beige and it was larger than the rest. Although the teacher sat with her back towards him, Matt knew that she was young. Her clothes were young: a short-sleeved beige jumper with a matching skirt that had ridden up well above her knees, probably because of the awkwardness of the way she was perched on a child's chair; the manner in which she leaned forward was young, one smooth hand pointing so that all the children could see an open book placed in the centre of the tables; and the way she shook her head was young, her collar length light brown hair flicking to one side before falling back into perfect position. Matt took all this in but he still stood over by the door and made no attempt to move forward.

'Well, go on then,' prompted George. 'I thought you wanted to see Miss Williams?'

The teacher, hearing George's distinctive voice, turned and glanced towards the door. She stood up and smiled at the visitor and Matt, feeling like the village idiot, nodded his head and grinned back.

She *was* young – about twenty-four, Matt guessed – and very attractive. The beige jumper had tightened as she stood up, defining her figure, and Matt consciously tried not to stare at her breasts. Her eyes were brown. He could see that across the classroom, brown and appealing, as if welcoming him with just a glance. He loved brown eyes. It had been Lydia's eyes that had attracted him to her and he still remembered the last look she had given him as she turned and walked away for the final time.

Miss Williams gave a few more instructions to the group she was working with and then walked across the classroom to deal with Matt. He really liked what he saw. How come his teachers had never looked like Miss Williams? In the few seconds it took her to approach, Matt had a flashback to the final year of his own primary school. Mrs Brunt! How he had hated that woman!

He could still picture her standing at the front of the class with her arms folded across a huge bosom. Her grey hair was permanently pinned into a tight bun at the back of her head and she had a dark moustache which twitched whenever she frowned. Matt seemed to remember that moustache twitching a great deal. How times had changed!

'Can I help you? Have you come to collect Lucy? Are you Lucy's dad?'

'No, no,' said Matt, quickly. He was aware that he was still grinning. 'I'm not anyone's dad. Well, not as far as I know!' He cringed and wished he hadn't made the last comment. 'I've come to fix your computer. I'm told you've got a problem?'

'Sorry,' said Miss Williams, 'I was expecting Lucy's dad. She's not been well, you see.' She indicated a sad little girl sitting alone near the sink, a plastic bucket on her knee. Her face was bright pink and she was making strange gurgling noises. 'The secretary's rung for her to be collected. Anyway, the computer trolley's in the library corner. It's a spare, really, for the children to use when they've finished their work. I'm sorry but you'll have to excuse me while I get on.'

'That's fine,' said Matt, and he stood and watched as the teacher made her way back to the group of children near the window.

'Go on then,' said George, who had been listening to every word, 'you know where it is.'

Matt had sorted the computer within five minutes. Once he'd removed the metal plate from the back of the stack, the loose connection was obvious. Matt grunted in satisfaction and was about to replace the plate when the delicious Miss Williams appeared to check his progress.

'Nothing too serious, I hope?' She flicked her hair again and her brown eyes widened in enquiry.

'It's a little tricky but I'll sort it out for you,' lied Matt. 'Bit out of date, this computer. You could do with replacing it.'

He took a small screwdriver from his black case and prodded around loosely in the back of the computer.

'It's happened before, you know,' announced a familiar voice. George had appeared at the teacher's side, exercise book in hand. 'The last fella said he'd fixed it.'

'Is he your minder?' enquired Matt.

'He doesn't miss much,' said Miss Williams, and she led him by the arm back to his table.

Matt watched them all the way and realised that it was jealousy he felt when he saw the teacher put her arm around George's shoulder and explain a piece of work to him.

He shook his head and looked back at the

computer. 'What's the point?' he thought, and he finished the job quickly and picked up his case.

I wonder what her first name is?

Matt leaned on the narrow shelf at the office window and let the thought meander through his mind. He was waiting for the secretary to return with his 'work completed' form signed.

'Melanie, or Melinda, maybe. She could be a Rachel. Yes, a Rachel would definitely have soft, brown eyes and a cute figure.'

Matt stared through the glass at the picture calendar of Snowdonia on the wall opposite. He toyed with the idea of asking the secretary to divulge Miss Williams' first name, but that would be too obvious. Besides, he didn't really want to engage the woman in any conversation that wasn't absolutely necessary. He'd made that mistake last time. Instead, he accepted the signed slip, wished the secretary well and headed back to his car.

Outside, the drizzle was heavier and the sky a darker, more depressing shade of grey. As Matt approached the car park, he noticed the blue van had not moved. It was there, blocking his exit, exactly where it had been half an hour ago.

'Shit!' muttered Matt, as he pulled up the collar on his jacket. 'Where the hell is he?'

And then Matt spotted a large pair of boots through the driver's side window. He approached the van and stared inside. The driver was sprawled out across the two front seats, cigarette in one hand, plastic flask top full of steaming liquid in the other.

Matt rapped on the window and the driver glanced up at him.

'Can you move it, please mate? You're blocking me in.'

The driver slowly raised an open hand to indicate five minutes.

'I've got another job to go to. You can't leave it here! Shift the bloody thing!'

The driver smiled and his hand changed shape to leave just two fingers moving ever so slowly upwards. He was a big man. Matt could see he was a big man. Besides, what difference would five minutes make? Matt turned away and clicked the remote to unlock his door.

Inside, he checked his job card. He had thought as much – Superior Fitted Kitchens of Chorlton-cum-Hardy. What could they possibly have done to their computer this time?

Chapter 2

32 Ashton Avenue, East Didsbury. Matt had never really understood why this cramped, narrow street consisting of sixty-eight red bricked terraced houses had been designated an avenue. Surely an avenue was wider and lined with trees? He had bought the house five years ago in the assumption that he would share it with Lydia. She had told him as much, promised him that they would do it up together. In fairness, she did move in with him for a couple of weeks – but then came the offer of a job in London. How could she turn it down? She was a struggling dancer looking for a break and a part in a West End musical couldn't be refused, even if it was only in the chorus line. She came back just once after the audition and that was to tell him she was leaving. Matt could still picture those brown eyes as she walked away for the last time. All that he was left with was a property that he was struggling to maintain and a mortgage that he couldn't really afford.

Five years on and he was still there, still struggling, still harbouring an unrealistic hope that one day Lydia would suddenly appear on his doorstep with her suitcase and that their lives would move forward together. He knew that it would not happen but he refused to let go of that thin thread of hope.

It was six-fifteen and pitch black. Matt turned the key in the front door and stumbled into the hallway. He would have to get that door fixed. It had been sticking for weeks. There was a free newspaper on the floor and he pushed it to one side with his foot so that it joined last week's free newspaper. Why did they bother? Full of adverts and lonely hearts pages. Now there was a thought – lonely hearts pages. Matt shook his head, flicked on the light and turned left into the living room. That's what he called it – a *living room*. It wasn't a lounge, it was a living room. He remembered his father, a proud Yorkshire man from Whitby who called a spade a bloody shovel, explaining to him that 'Posh people 'ave lounges whilst the likes of us 'ave living rooms'.

Matt took off his jacket, damp and musty from the day's drizzle, and tossed it over the back of a chair before flopping down on the sofa. He stared at the blank TV screen for a moment and his weary reflection stared back at him.

'Bloody marvellous,' he said out loud. 'Another day of your life gone and what have you achieved, Matthew Hudson? The same as every other day – absolutely nothing . . .'

He had got into the habit of talking to himself. He did it all the time, especially when at home and if he addressed his comments to the TV screen, it was as if someone was actually listening to him. The problem was that he never got a reply. Just lately he had begun to talk to the mirror in his car. At least it helped to relieve the boredom.

'What shall we do this evening, then? I know – let's watch some crap on television and then have an early night. After all, tomorrow's the first day of the rest of your life. Bollocks! Depressing, or what?'

The TV didn't answer.

The phone rang and it made Matt jump. Why did he always do that? He never used to jump when the phone rang. Matt picked it up.

'Hello, Hudson's house.'

'Matt, it's me! How's it going?'

Matt looked away and grimaced. Why did Beano insist on ringing him every single evening? Why didn't he give him a break?

'It's going fine, Beano. How's things with you?'

'Mustn't complain. Skived off work a couple of hours early today. Developed a bad back, if you know what I mean. I think it'll be better about next Tuesday. Listen, do you fancy a pint in The Old Cock later? It'll drive me mad sitting in all evening. I'll be bloody well talking to myself next!'

Matt put his hand over the receiver and groaned. He should have been prepared. He should have had his excuse ready. He should have left the answer phone switched on.

'I – I don't know, Beano. I'm a bit short of cash and . . .'

'Oh, come on! You're not telling me a computer whiz kid like you can't afford one pint? What else were you going to do?'

'Go on then! Just for an hour or so, eh?'

'Fantastic! I'll see you in there about nine o'clock.'

The phone went dead and Matt stared at the receiver. Somehow that early night seemed suddenly attractive.

The pub was pretty crowded for a Wednesday evening. The Old Cock Inn was always crowded, usually with students from the local college. Matt leaned on the bar and watched a group of young people clustered around two round tables, drinking and generally talking in voices several decibels too loud. They had obviously been in the pub for some time. The tables were cluttered with empty glasses and bottles, the glasses stacked high and precariously balanced. There was only just enough room for their mobile phones.

Why did students always look the same? It was a timeless look. That group, with their sloppy jumpers and their shirts outside their trousers, could have been sitting there ten years ago when Matt was a student himself. They probably had been judging by the number of glasses they had accumulated.

Matt's thoughts were interrupted by the arrival of Beano. He bustled through the door, paused for a moment and then headed purposefully towards the bar.

'I've got you one in,' said Matt. 'Thought you might be desperate.'

'Cheers mate!' And Beano picked up his pint and downed half of it in four great gulps. He wiped his mouth with the back of his hand, let out a deep belch and said, 'Christ! I needed that!'

'There's a table in the corner,' said Matt, indicating with a nod of his head. 'Well away from this lot, eh?'

'Good move,' agreed Beano, and he picked up his pint and set off for the far corner of the pub.

There was no way Beano could be described as a fashion icon. Matt had known him since his student days when they had been in adjacent rooms at the Didsbury Hall of Residence. Beano had never changed – he had just got bigger and heavier, the result of years of bitter drinking and an appetite like an army's. Matt reckoned he only had two pairs of trousers – one brown pair and one khaki. He would wear the same pair for weeks until they were so stained with kebab and curry that even Beano realised they were ready for the laundry. In fairness, he did have several shirts, all the same style, just different colours. He obviously couldn't decide how to wear his shirts because they were invariably half in and half out of his trousers. The only consistent thing about them was that they were always crumpled. Beano didn't have a hairstyle. His thick, brown hair just sat there on top of his head and fell where it wanted. He was one of the few people that Matt knew who actually looked worse when he washed his hair – but that didn't happen too often.

Beano had studied drama at college but the nearest he'd got to a career in acting was his job building and shifting sets at Granada studios. He was, however, sometimes called upon as an extra and the discerning viewer could often spot him in the background at The Rovers Return, brown trousers, shirt half in, half out. He fitted in perfectly. Beano was clearly getting bored building sets and, as a result, he had developed a recurring back problem.

Matt had noticed that he seemed to be moving pretty freely as he entered the pub and, as he settled into his seat in the corner, shuffling around to get more comfortable, there was not much evidence of a bad back.

'Bloody students,' observed Beano. 'Where do they get the money? It's people like us funding them, you know.'

'Haven't you heard of student loans, Beano? Most of these kids will be in debt for the next twenty years. Anyway, I don't remember us ever going short of something to drink when we were at college.'

'We didn't sit there with our bloody mobile phones, sipping from poncy little bottles of vodka mixers. I don't know what's happened to this place.'

'Listen to you talking! You're beginning to sound old, Beano!'

'I *am* old, Matt. I'm twenty-eight years old. Twenty-nine next month. Christ, another year and I'll be thirty!' Beano picked up his pint and took another three great gulps. 'You know the sad thing, Matt? I'm really beginning to *feel* old. I look at these young kids in here and I wonder where the last ten years have gone. Why do we keep coming here? It's depressing!'

'We keep coming here because we've always come here,' said Matt. 'And we keep coming here because we like a good moan. Besides, every other pub in Didsbury's full of students too – all looking the same and clutching their mobile phones.'

'Well it's bloody depressing,' confirmed Beano, and he drained the rest of his glass and banged it down on the table.

Across the room, one of the students

rose unsteadily to his feet, a full pint of lager in his hand. The others began to clap in rhythm as he raised the glass to his lips. Two of the girls picked up bottles and banged them on the table as he began to drink. The clapping got louder and faster as the lager disappeared down the student's throat and there was a loud, disorderly cheer as he banged the empty glass down on the table and sank back into his chair, trickles of frothy lager dribbling from his mouth.

'Bloody prat,' muttered Beano. 'Do you realise we're paying taxes to put him through university. What's the point?'

'You used to do it,' Matt reminded his friend. 'It used to be your party piece when you'd had a few!'

'Not with lager, it didn't. I used to drink bitter. I've always drunk bitter.'

'Yes – and you've turned into a bitter old bugger! Perhaps you should change to vodka mixers!'

Beano managed a thin smile but he didn't reply.

The students settled down to more serious drinking and, as their conversation became more and more slurred, Matt lost interest. While Beano was at the bar, he studied the other drinkers in the pub. They were mostly young, groups of three or four, some of them clutching books or files. An older man, probably in his late forties, sat with a young girl at a table for two, a battered brown leather briefcase at his feet. They were deep in conversation, the girl doing most of the listening, twisting a thin strand of her long, blonde hair round and round her fingers.

'Probably a lecturer,' muttered Matt. 'Bet he thinks he's on to a good thing.'

Now he was talking to himself in pubs. That was worrying.

The Old Cock was divided into three rooms. Matt and Beano always sat in the main part of the pub. It was the largest of the bars and there were more people to watch. A second bar housed a huge TV screen, which either showed live football games or belted out MTV. The third bar was smaller and was usually used as an overspill. For some reason it was known as the Canal Bar. Matt hadn't a clue why, for as far as he knew, there were no canals anywhere near Didsbury.

Matt was aware that there were customers present in this smaller third bar but he couldn't quite see them. He glanced up to see Beano talking earnestly to the barmaid. Some things never changed. Why couldn't he just bring the pints back?

Matt leaned sideways in an effort to catch a glimpse of those in the Canal Bar. He could see two girls, both with pints of bitter, leaning forward slightly over a round table. They looked older than the students, as if they had worked for a few years and had seen a little more of life. The nearest had short, cropped brown hair that was streaked with red. Matt could see that her left ear was pierced several times, the full length of her lobe, and decorated with different sized rings. She had a silver stud in her nose. He couldn't help but wonder what else was pierced. She was holding an unlit cigarette, probably waiting to go outside for a smoke. She seemed to be doing most of the talking.

Her friend was plump. That was the first word that came into Matt's mind. He considered it for a few moments and wondered if the description was too kind. She was wearing a large, purple sloppy jumper but it couldn't disguise the fact that she had a weight problem. She appeared to be munching her way through a giant bag of barbecue beef crisps, which she washed down every so often with a swig of bitter.

Beano reappeared with the pints.

'You took your time,' said Matt. 'Thought you didn't love me anymore.'

'New girl behind the bar,' explained Beano. 'You've got to get on the right side of these people, you know.'

'I don't understand why civilised men and women choose to get their bodies pierced.' Matt nodded towards the Canal Bar where the red haired girl was still dominating the conversation.

'I find it quite attractive, actually,' said

Beano. He took a gulp of his pint and wiped his mouth. 'I think it's the pain factor. Think what she'd go through for you!'

'She looks like a curtain rail,' observed Matt. 'What's attractive about a curtain rail?'

'I'll tell you what,' said Beano, 'I'll have her and you can have her friend.'

'I think I'll go for a pee, instead,' said Matt. 'I can still just about manage that.'

Matt edged out of his seat and made his way across the bar towards the toilets. He glanced into the Canal Bar as he passed and stopped in his tracks. There, sitting opposite the red haired girl, was Miss Williams – the delicious Miss Williams from St Gregory's School. She had two empty glasses in her hands and she was just getting up from her seat. He recognised her straight away. She had the same jumper on but had swapped her skirt for a tight fitting pair of denims. She passed a final comment to her friends and then walked out into the main bar. Matt was still standing there, directly in her way.

'Hello,' she said, and she smiled with her deep, brown eyes. 'A1 Computers, isn't it? You were in school today?'

'That's right,' said Matt. 'Everything all right, I hope?'

'Everything's fine!' said Miss Williams. 'You would have heard from our Head by now if it wasn't.'

'I've – er, I've not seen you in here before. Do you come here often?'

Matt cringed inside. Had he really just used that line?

'Quite a bit,' replied Miss Williams, 'especially when I've had a bad day.' She nodded towards her friends. 'They're my flat mates.'

'Right,' said Matt. 'Great. Well, I'm just going for a p – pint.'

'Me too,' said Miss Williams. 'We're blocking the way a bit here, aren't we?'

They moved towards the bar, Matt desperately trying to think of something else to say.

'My name's Matt, by the way.' He was pleased with that. It was an obvious way forward.

'Laura,' she replied, smiling. 'I'm Laura.'

'Laura,' repeated Matt. 'I'd not thought of that one.'

Laura gave him a puzzled look but he didn't respond so she moved on.

'You live locally, then?'

'I live in East Didsbury,' said Matt, 'walking distance from this place. What about you?'

'Chorlton,' replied Laura. 'I share a flat with those two. I'm looking for a place of my own. Need a bit more space.'

'I know what you mean,' said Matt, and he immediately thought that he could give her all the space she needed. 'I live on my own,' he continued. 'I like it like that. Not that I wouldn't I mean . . . I like the space.'

Matt cringed inside. It wasn't going well.

The barmaid walked over and stood in front of them. She didn't say anything; she just stood there.

'Can I get you a drink?' said Matt.

'It's OK, I'm buying for the three of us.'

'Oh – right.' He was aware that he was grinning again.

Laura ordered her drinks – a glass of white wine and two pints of bitter. Matt guessed that the bitters were for the red head and the fat one.

He hesitated for a moment and then he said: 'Maybe we could get together for a drink some time? If you'd like to, that is?'

'That would be good,' said Laura, picking a pint up in each hand. 'Why don't you give me a ring?'

Matt couldn't believe it. His heart surged.

'I'll do that. I'll give you a ring – promise.'

Laura smiled again and then walked away with the two pints, leaving her glass of wine on the bar. Matt thought about taking it over for her but he decided that might look too pushy. Instead, he turned away and continued towards the gents.

'Yes!' he said, as he unzipped his trousers. 'Nice one!' And the student in the next trap gave him a strange glance.

Matt rinsed his hands and stared at the Durex machine as he dried them.

'Not just yet,' he said out loud, 'but with a bit of luck I might be back soon!'

The student's mobile phone went off and he cursed as he peed all over his trouser leg.

Chapter 3

It was the following morning before Matt realised that he hadn't got her phone number. He wasn't going to let this one go and he decided that the only solution was to ring Laura at work. By mid morning Matt was between jobs. He pulled over into a side road and dialled the school on his mobile. Maybe he could catch Laura on her morning break.

The phone rang briefly and then a brusque voice announced: 'St Gregory's School, Mrs Nelson speaking.'

Shit! It was the Headteacher. Perhaps she wouldn't recognise his voice.

'Oh, good morning. I was wondering whether I could have a word with Miss Williams, please?'

'I'll see if she's still in the staffroom. Who's calling, please?'

'Mr Hudson, A1 Computers.' He had no choice. He had to admit it. Perhaps she would assume it was a follow-up call to his visit.

There was a minute's pause before Laura

picked up the phone.

'Hi, it's Matt. Matthew Hudson. You remember – we spoke in the pub last night.'

'Yes, I remember,' said Laura, and she waited for Matt to continue.

'I didn't take your phone number and I promised to ring.' He was nervous. His heart was beating too quickly, which made him rush his words. Ridiculous! He was only talking to her on the phone.

'I wondered if you were free Saturday evening? We could meet for that drink?'

'Saturday? Yes, I think Saturday would be OK.'

Laura sounded unsure, or was she just taken by surprise?

'Great! Why don't we meet at the Italian Bar in Didsbury? We can get something to eat as well. Does eight-thirty sound all right?'

'I'll be there,' said Laura. 'I'll have to go now. I'm due back in class. Thanks for ringing.'

The phone went dead and Matt stared at it for a few moments.

'Yes!' he said, and he clenched his fist in triumph. 'Yes! Yes! Yes!'

A young mother walked by with a pushchair. She gave him a strange look and hurried away from the parked car as quickly as she could.

Chapter 4

The university years had been a big disappointment for Matt. He had arrived in Manchester full of expectation, anticipating three years of social activity coupled with an awakening of sexual experience. He had been so frustrated in Whitby. As a teenager, he'd had friends who were girls but he had never had the confidence to get himself a proper girlfriend during his time at the Grammar School and, although the beach could be interesting in summer, Whitby was hardly the centre of the universe out of season, except, perhaps when the Goths arrived at the end of October. Being an only child, his parents were disappointed that he wanted to move so far away from home, his father assuming that he would work the fishing boats, despite having passed the entrance exam for the Grammar School.

He met Beano on his very first day at university. Matt had just dumped his cases in his room at the hall of residence when Beano poked his head around the door.

'Don't suppose you've got any sugar?' he

said. 'I can't drink coffee without sugar. It tastes bloody awful!'

'I have somewhere,' said Matt. 'My mum packed some in a Tupperware box. Come on in a minute while I look for it.'

Beano had not stopped bothering him ever since. They went out drinking that first evening, together with Sparrow, a tall skinny boy who had a room further along the corridor. They got horribly drunk, all three of them, and Beano was violently sick in his room. Boy could he vomit! Luckily, each room had a metal waste paper bin that had a good capacity and didn't leak.

Matt's success with the girls was limited, mostly due to his lack of confidence, and he soon began to get disillusioned. There was a ginger haired girl from Wales, Bronwyn Hughes, who was in the same IT Studies group as Matt. No matter how much he tried to avoid her, she always seemed to get on the next computer station to him. It wasn't the fright of ginger hair and mess of freckles that put him off, it was her incessant, laborious, mindless chatter. Bronwyn never shut up. Matt knew all about her family, her friends at home, her house in St Asaph, her school, her pet rabbits . . . it was relentless. In the evenings, she would seek him out in the University bar and carry on from where she had left off earlier.

Beano found it hilarious. 'Why don't you give her one?' he suggested, as they sat in Matt's room late one night, drinking coffee and listening to The Stone Roses. 'All that talk about rabbits is a hint, you know! At least it would shut her up for a few minutes!'

'I doubt it,' said Matt, seriously. 'She'd gasp and pant and describe the Eisteddfod!'

Like most students, they had taken to serious drinking. Beano could pour a pint down his throat in a matter of seconds and he demonstrated the skill to anyone who would buy him a replacement pint. Even Sparrow put on weight and by the end of the second term his nickname was inappropriate.

The only fly in the ointment was the work they were expected to complete. Consistently late nights resulted in even later mornings, which meant that Matt was missing lectures and seminars. It therefore came as no surprise either to him or to anyone else that he failed his first year quite miserably. It did, however, bring him a sharp stab of reality. If he didn't buckle down to it and pass the August re-sits it would be back to Whitby for a life on the fishing boats. As a result, Matt locked himself in his room for weeks, even refusing Beano's enticements to an end of year drinking binge. Instead, he downed gallons of black coffee and managed to scrape through to the second year, where the whole cycle was repeated.

Matt had seen the advert for A1 Computers on the University notice board and he had amazed himself when he landed the job at his very first interview. It did his confidence a power of good. The job was fine, at first. The company was based in Didsbury so he wouldn't have to move away from the area. He was young and reasonably enthusiastic, he enjoyed travelling around and, for the first time in his life, he had spare money in his pocket. He even subsidised Beano for a while, sharing a flat with him while he hunted for work. However, it only took a few months for Matt to realise just how tedious his job really was. He would get the same callouts to the same places to service the same faults. But there was nothing else he could do. He would have to stick with it.

His biggest mistake was sharing a flat with Beano. Matt was untidy but Beano was a beast. The first thing that greeted Matt when he arrived home from work was the smell. He would open the front door and it would hit him. It wasn't one, particular, distinctive smell, it was a mixture of smells, an amalgam of socks, toilets and Beano's Weetabix curry. That was his speciality, Weetabix curry. He would buy a pound and a half of mince, an onion and a jar of Madras paste on a Monday morning. He would cook it on a Monday afternoon, adding half a packet of Weetabix to thicken it, and it would last him through to Friday. Weekends were different; at weekends he would make a chilli with more mince, baked beans and a tin of chopped tomatoes.

It got to the point where Matt felt physically sick when he walked through the door, so he confronted Beano with a list of demands. In fairness, things did improve. Beano used a milder curry paste, cleaned the toilet once a week and bought a can of air freshener.

Eventually, however, Matt gave Beano an ultimatum – find work or find somewhere else to live. It was at that point that Beano got a job with a telesales company promoting fitted kitchens and bedrooms. He lasted three weeks; his telephone manner was dreadful.

Meeting Lydia had been a turning point in Matt's life. He had been to a callout at the Palace Theatre in Manchester and he was sitting with a coffee in Sam's Bar on Oxford Road, before returning to his car. He had noticed her the moment she had walked through the door. Tall, very slim with collar length brown hair and deep brown eyes. Matt had always loved brown eyes. He still remembered the puppy he had as a child and Lydia's eyes were every bit as wide and appealing. Matt was transfixed. He held his coffee cup mid way between the table and his lips and he stared at her as she placed her order. He was still staring as she picked up her tray and began to walk in his direction, glancing around for a free table. He smiled as she approached and, to his amazement, she smiled back – at least he thought she did. And then it happened. Someone had dropped a piece of cake on the floor. She trod on a blob of cream and her foot shot from under her. Matt froze in horror as both the tray and the brown-eyed girl crashed to the floor before his very eyes.

He was there in a flash, helping her up and offering sympathy.

'Are you OK? Nothing broken, is there – apart from the coffee mug?'

'No, no – I'm fine,' she said, although her voice was trembling. 'Just my pride that's hurt. I should have been looking where I was going.'

He was in quickly, surprised at his confidence. 'Come and sit down for a minute. Let me get you another coffee.' And he was at the counter before she had a chance to refuse. 'I'm Matt,' he said, as he rejoined her at the table. 'No sugar. I hope that's correct?'

'Lydia,' she replied, smiling with her eyes. 'And no sugar's fine.'

Matt sat down opposite her, reached for his cream doughnut and realised with horror that it was missing from his plate. The remnants of it were still on Lydia's shoe. He picked up his coffee instead and asked, 'Do you work round here?'

'Just down the road,' replied Lydia. 'I'm at the Palace Theatre.'

'Really?' said Matt. 'I've just been there myself. Are you in the office or on ticket sales?'

She smiled at him for a moment, stirred her coffee and said, 'Neither. I'm appearing in the show. I'm a dancer.'

Matt could have kicked himself. 'Sorry. It's me who's put my foot in it this time!'

They bought another coffee each and stayed there for an hour, until Lydia said, 'I'll really have to get back. Rehearsals start in ten minutes. It's been good talking to you.'

'Can I see you again?' said Matt. The words were out there before he realised what he was saying, before he had a chance to get nervous.

'All right,' said Lydia. 'I'd like that. After the show tomorrow evening. You can buy me something a bit stronger.' And she put her hand in her pocket and pulled out a fifty pence coin. 'Get yourself another doughnut,' she said, slapping it on the table in front of Matt. 'I'd hate to see you go hungry!'

It was all so long ago. Beano had kept on the flat for a while when Matt had moved into Ashton Avenue, Lydia had left him for a career in London and all that remained was his tedious job with A1 Computers. The same calls to the same places to service the same faults. Until, of course, he had got the call to visit St Gregory's Primary School. Was that going to be another turning point in his life?

Chapter 5

Matt had spent an hour deciding what to wear. The trousers were fine; plain black went with anything. It was the shirt that had caused him a problem. Short sleeved or long sleeved? He decided short sleeved. His arms weren't bad, a bit thin but attractively hairy, he thought. That had narrowed it down a bit – but which one should he go for? He tried on a blue striped shirt that had no collar but the more he stared in the mirror the more convinced he became that his neck was too long. Like an ostrich, he thought, long and scrawny. The orange one was hideous. He had bought it cheap in the summer sales and only worn it once. The dark green one was probably his favourite but he wasn't sure the curry stain had washed out properly. Eventually, he settled for his maroon shirt with the button down collar. He wore the shirt outside his trousers and, when he checked in the mirror, he was pretty well satisfied.

An hour and a half later, as he stood outside the Italian Bar, he wasn't so convinced. Maybe the green one suited him better, or perhaps he should have gone for long sleeves. It was mid November, after all. He shivered and shuffled around uncomfortably.

It was eight-fifteen and he realised he was too early. He could be standing in the cold for another half hour if she was late. What if she didn't come at all? He glanced nervously up and down the road, confidence ebbing away by the minute.

Laura arrived just after eight-thirty. A battered Ford Fiesta pulled up at the kerb and she climbed out of the passenger side. She waved at the red head and shouted, 'Thanks, Dina!' as the car pulled back into the traffic and disappeared.

'Hope you haven't been waiting long?' she said to Matt. 'You did say eight-thirty, didn't you?'

'I've only just arrived,' lied Matt. All of a sudden he didn't feel cold anymore. 'And yes – I did say eight-thirty. Let's go inside, shall we?'

The bar was busy for early evening. This was the New Didsbury, with its continental bars and pavement cafés, a cosmopolitan Didsbury that had developed in the past decade or so to cater for the growing number of wealthy commuters who had bought property in the area. The students, too, had taken to the new eating places and, as a result, the area was still developing, with more bars planned and work continuing on new executive property conversions.

Matt wasn't sure why he had suggested the Italian Bar. He had never even set foot inside the place. However, he acted as if he was a regular and the Italian waiter seemed to play along, speaking to him as if he had known him for years.

They sat at a table for two near the window, where they could watch the evening develop as Didsbury Village came to life.

Laura was easy to talk to and Matt felt relaxed in her company. He was glad he had chosen the maroon shirt, as she was wearing a green, open neck shirt over loose, black trousers. It wouldn't have done for them both to wear green.

They ordered from the Italian menu, she cannelloni and he a spaghetti carbonara. They shared a portion of garlic bread between them and Matt ordered a bottle of house red, a very acceptable Chianti. Matt thought he might have made a mistake when he began to eat his spaghetti but he coped pretty well and she only laughed at him on a couple of occasions, when it trailed out of his mouth, causing him to lean forward over his bowl and stab at it with his fork and spoon.

Conversation was easy and the more the Chianti went down, the easier the conversation became.

'Tell me about yourself?' said Matt, as he indicated to the waiter for a second bottle.

'What do you want to know?' She sipped her wine and stared straight at him.

'Everything. Where are you from? What do you like doing? How come you're here in Didsbury? Tell me everything.'

'My family live in Rivington, not too far away, really. I've got one younger sister and a brother who works as a journalist in London. I suppose I'm the boring one – I went in for teaching. I trained here in Didsbury and I was lucky enough to get a job in the area. I've been at St Gregory's for three years now. I really like it there and I get on well with the staff but I suppose I'll be ready for a move before too long.'

'I don't think you're at all boring,' said Matt. The second bottle of Chianti arrived and he refilled the glasses. He was aware that he was already light-headed and it was a good feeling.

Laura smiled. 'I don't live at home,' she continued, 'I share a house with Dina and Meg. It was Dina who dropped me off outside the restaurant.'

'Are they teachers, too?' asked Matt. He realised that his glass of wine was going down far too quickly.

'Dina works at a High School in Salford,' said Laura. 'It's pretty tough, I think, but she seems to like it. I met her at university. We were on teaching practice together. Meg's a nurse. We needed someone else to share the house and Meg was first to answer the advert.'

'You said you're looking for a place of your own? Why do you want to move out?'

Laura giggled and flicked her brown hair. 'Sex,' she said, suddenly, and Matt nearly choked on his wine. 'Too much sex. I can't stand it!'

Matt's eyes widened and he shuffled uneasily in his seat.

'Not me,' she explained, quickly. 'It's Dina. She never stops! She has what you might call an unusual taste in boyfriends – and girlfriends, I'm afraid. It's embarrassing.'

'That's a relief!' said Matt, and he took a large gulp of Chianti.

'It's not funny if you live with her,' continued Laura. 'We have our own rooms but – honestly! The noises! Meg doesn't seem to bother – she just turns up the television or listens to her iPod – but it's beginning to get to me. I need some privacy . . . Anyway, I feel at a disadvantage. You know everything about me and I know nothing at all about you.'

'Where do I begin?' said Matt, and he desperately searched his brain for something interesting to tell her about his life.

They left the bar at eleven-thirty. Matt had rung for a taxi and the two of them climbed into the back and sank into the soft seat. Matt had just assumed that he would see her home.

'Chorlton, please,' said Laura. 'Just across

from the bus station.'

The taxi driver nodded and the cab pulled away.

They were sitting close together and Laura leaned against Matt and rested her head on his shoulder.

'It's been a good evening,' she said. 'Thanks for asking me.'

Matt wasn't sure what to say. As a way of answering, he put his arm around her and pulled her closer. After a few minutes, he said, 'You'll come out with me again, then?'

'I'd like that,' said Laura, quietly. 'I'd like that very much.'

She turned her face towards him, waiting for him to react and so, he kissed her, there in the back of the taxi, softly at first and then more intensely, his hand in her hair, pulling her forward.

Matt didn't go into the house with her but he did remember to get her phone number. The taxi had driven off, leaving him standing on the pavement in the cold November air, staring at the door to Laura's flat. Why hadn't he kept the taxi? He was freezing in that short-sleeved shirt.

Matt walked across towards the bus station. In truth, it wasn't much of a bus station. It could only take four buses at any one time. It was more like a lay-by. The station was practically deserted. To its right was Chorlton Police Station, equally small, with one police car parked outside. An Afro-Caribbean youth was waiting for a bus at one of the shelters, his hands in his pockets, a baseball cap the wrong way round on his head.

As Matt watched, a group of white kids came around the corner from behind the police station. They were loud, laughing and shouting and pushing each other around. Matt thought nothing of it at first, but, later, when he had time to reflect, he recalled there were about six of them altogether, including at least two girls. One of the girls could hardly walk. She was staggering and chanting some unrecognisable words, two of her friends doing their best to support her.

The Afro-Caribbean kid took one look at them and started to walk away. But it was too late. They had seen him and they charged after him, leaving the girl to fend for herself. They were on him in seconds, grabbing his hooded jumper and pulling him backwards. Matt couldn't believe his eyes. They were laying into him for no apparent reason. He was on the ground, his hands trying to protect his head and they were kicking him. He was shouting out but they didn't stop. They were right outside the police station and they were kicking him.

Matt raced across the road yelling as loud as he could. One last kick went in and the youths ran off, the drunken girl staggering after them as best she could. Matt could hear them sneering and laughing as they ran off.

The Afro-Caribbean youth was still on the floor with his hands over his head. His knuckles were bleeding.

Matt crouched next to him and said, 'Are you all right? What the fuck was that about?'

The kid lowered his hands slowly and pulled himself into a sitting position. He was no more than sixteen years old. He was shaking, shivering with shock rather than from the cold. His lip was cut and it was already swollen but his hands seemed to have taken most of the blows.

'I'm all right. Thanks. I'm all right.'

'Can you stand up?' Matt helped him to his feet. 'Do you know those bastards?'

'I'm not sure.' The kid was grimacing and holding his side. 'I might know one of them.'

'I'll come to the police station with you,' said Matt. 'I got a good look at them. I can give a description'

'I'm not goin' in,' said the kid. 'There's no point. Just leave it, right? Thanks for your help – but just leave it.'

And he moved away, still holding his side, leaving Matt to wipe a bloodstained hand on his maroon shirt.

Chapter 6

About an hour later the kid tried to enter his house quietly but he was aching all over. He knew he was late home and his father would go mad if he caught him sneaking in. Maybe he could get up to his bedroom without being heard. Grimacing with pain, he pulled off his hooded top and dropped it by the front door. Everywhere was quiet. The house was in darkness. He wondered, for a moment, whether to get a glass of water from the kitchen but he thought better of it. Instead, he took a deep breath and placed one foot on the bottom stair. The lights went on immediately and his father's stern face stared down at him from above.

'What time do you call this, boy? Where have you been?' The voice was harsh, almost accusing.

'I'm sorry, Father. I missed the last bus. I had to walk.' It hurt him to talk. There was a stabbing pain on the right side of his ribs with every breath he took.

His father advanced down the stairs towards him.

'Look at the state of you, Linton! What's happened to you?'

'It's nothing, Father. I've just been messing around . . . with the boys.'

'Don't lie to me, Linton! You've been in a fight.' He stared at Linton's bloodied mouth and grabbed one of the boy's hands, frowning when he saw the grazed and swollen knuckles. 'You need to get some ice on those swellings, boy.'

'It wasn't my fault,' said Linton, grasping his side. 'Some white kids at the bus station . . .'

'I don't want to know!' interrupted his father, firmly. 'I didn't bring you up to fight, Linton. You're in with the wrong crowd.'

A young girl of about seven crept onto the landing and peered down through the bars.

'But I was on my own,' protested Linton. 'That was the problem; they saw me on my own at the bus station. An older guy stepped in to help me.'

'You're getting involved with the wrong crowd,' continued his father, ignoring the boy's explanation, 'and you'll end up in trouble! Serious trouble! Do you understand me, boy?'

'I understand,' said Linton, in the hope that it would shut his father up.

'Is he gonna get grounded?' said a voice from the top of the stairs. 'It's not fair if he doesn't get grounded!'

'Get back to bed, Melissa!' snapped her

father. 'This is none of your business!'

Linton glared up the stairs towards his sister, who screwed up her face and pulled tongues at him before scurrying off into her bedroom.

'You take note of what I say, boy,' continued his father, placing a firm hand on Linton's arm. 'I want you to make something of your life, not waste it like I did at your age.'

'I'm listening,' said Linton, and he pulled away and started up the stairs, grimacing with pain as he took the first step. 'I'm hearing what you say Father.'

Chapter 7

Matt hadn't been able to get Laura out of his mind. He had turned up for work on Monday as usual but she was constantly in his thoughts. He scanned the job lists, desperately hoping that the computers had crashed at St Gregory's School. On Tuesday lunchtime he toyed with the idea of ringing her at school but he decided against it. After all, he didn't want her to think he was desperate.

By Tuesday evening he *was* desperate and he made up his mind that he would ring her the moment he got home from work. Matt picked up a takeaway from the Chinese in Didsbury Village and he rehearsed his words as he drove the short distance back to Ashton Avenue.

'Hi, Laura – it's Matt here. Sorry I've not been in touch for a few days but I've been really busy at work.'

No, that didn't sound right. She would think he viewed his work as more important than contacting her. He tried again.

'Hi, Laura. This is Matthew Hudson. We had an Italian together the other evening.'

That was worse. *We had an Italian together.* It sounded like a perverted sexual experience. He would have to do better than that.

He was still practising as he forced his way through the front door, almost dropping his takeaway as the door jammed and jarred in the swollen frame. He really would have to get that door fixed. Matt was surprised to see his answerphone flashing. Nobody ever left him a message. He didn't really need an answerphone. It occasionally came in handy when he wanted to avoid Beano. He would put it on in the evening and pretend he wasn't in. Matt stared at the red flashing light for a few moments before picking up the handset and hitting the playback button.

It was Laura! He recognised the voice immediately and his heart jumped. She had taken the time to ring him and she had left a message when she couldn't get through. Matt was so astonished that he completely missed the message. He hit the button again and concentrated on the words.

The message was short and to the point:

'Hello, Matt – it's Laura here. I really enjoyed the other evening. I've been waiting for you to ring. Listen, I've got a couple of tickets for The Royal Exchange this Friday evening. Give me a call if you're free. Bye!'

Matt played it again just to make sure he'd heard it correctly. *I've been waiting for you to ring.* That's what the message said – *I've been waiting for you to ring!*

'Yess–ss!' he said out loud. 'I've cracked it! I hate the bloody theatre – but who cares!'

Later that evening Beano came around. Matt was still in a state of euphoria when the doorbell rang and he couldn't hide his disappointment when he jerked open the front door to see Beano standing there with an inane grin on his face.

'Oh, it's you,' said Matt, making no move to invite Beano inside. 'What d'you want?'

'What d'you want?' repeated Beano. 'That's not very nice, is it? I've come round to brighten up your sad little life and that's the sort of greeting I get! Well – are you going to let me in, or what?'

Matt stood to one side and Beano pushed past.

'You need to get that door fixed,' he said, stepping over the free newspapers that still lay in the hallway. 'It's been like that for weeks!'

Matt scowled but decided not to comment as he forced the door back into the frame and then followed Beano through into the living room.

'There's a funny smell in here,' said Beano, sniffing the air. 'I mean – even stranger than usual.'

'Yes, well I've had a takeaway,' explained

Matt, pointing towards the arm of the couch where a polystyrene tray was balanced, still containing the greasy remnants of Matt's chicken chow mein. 'Anything else you want to criticise?'

'A bit touchy, aren't we?' said Beano, sitting down heavily at the opposite end of the couch. 'Had a bad day, have we?'

'As a matter of fact I've had a very good day,' said Matt. 'Or at least a good end to the day.'

Beano leaned forward. 'Tell me more,' he said. 'Have you had a call out to some posh rich bitch who needs a good overhaul?'

'Not exactly,' said Matt, slowly, 'but you could say a window of opportunity has opened up.'

'A window of opportunity!' mimicked Beano. 'You're spending too much time with computers! *A window of opportunity!* You've pulled, haven't you! After all this time, you've pulled! I hope you can remember what to do! Who's the lucky lady?'

'No-one you know,' said Matt, defensively. 'Just someone I met through work. Her name's Laura. She's a teacher. I'm going to the theatre with her on Friday night.'

'The theatre!' stammered Beano, and he laughed out loud. 'You hate the bloody theatre! You've always hated the theatre! Anyway, I thought you were coming out drinking with me

on Friday night? We always go down to The Old Cock on Fridays.'

'Sorry, mate,' said Matt, with a smug grin on his face. 'Tempting though it is – I've had a better offer!'

It was a modern day version of *Hamlet*. Laura had got the tickets on a free promotion from school and she was waiting for Matt as the taxi drew up outside her flat in Chorlton.

'This is a bit extravagant,' she said, as she climbed into the back beside Matt. It'll cost a fortune both ways.'

'Don't worry about it,' said Matt. 'I thought we could go for a drink afterwards. Besides, I drive around all week. It makes a nice change to have a chauffeur.'

They chatted about the Italian restaurant and about St Gregory's School and even about computers and they were pulling up outside The Royal Exchange before they had even realised they were in the city centre.

'They won't be the best seats,' said Laura, as they climbed the stairs to the circle. 'We're obviously up in the gods somewhere.'

Matt smiled politely and followed in her footsteps. He didn't like heights. As a child, he'd fallen from a tree while he was on holiday in Wales and he'd been scared of heights ever since.

They were three rows from the back, right in the middle seats, between a bald man in a green anorak on one side and two arty looking twenty-somethings on the other. It was a long way down to the stage.

'Do you know *Hamlet*?' asked Laura, as they settled into their seats.

'Not personally,' replied Matt. He realised himself that it wasn't funny. 'I'm familiar with the plot but I've never studied the play.'

'This is supposed to be a bit different,' explained Laura. 'It's set in modern times in the Middle East. It's had really good reviews.'

Matt slipped a bit further down into his seat as the lights dimmed. He had a feeling it was going to be a long couple of hours.

It wasn't easy to follow. The costumes were a mixture of Arabic and military and the scenery resembled a bomb site – ruined buildings and rubble. The longer it went on the more it was passing over Matt's head. He could feel his eyes growing heavier and he was struggling to stop himself from yawning. He was willing it to finish. He didn't care what the hell happened to Hamlet, or to any of the other characters, for that matter.

And then disaster struck. It was a key moment in the performance. The King and Polonius had just made their exit from the stage and Hamlet was in position for his *To be, or not to be* soliloquy. The audience was tense with expectancy – and Matt's mobile phone went off. It sang out into the silence. It was playing *The William Tell Overture.*

Matt jerked in his seat as if he had been shot. Laura's eyes widened but she stared straight ahead as if she didn't know him. Heads turned and the action on stage froze in time. Hamlet looked as if he'd seen another ghost! Matt fumbled desperately in his inside pocket and pulled out the offending demon. Now it was even louder. The sound seemed to fill the whole theatre, echoing around the auditorium like a bad dream. He juggled the phone in his hands for a moment, prodding frantically towards the off button until the sound died as suddenly as it had begun, leaving only his embarrassment to fill the vacuum.

'To be, or not to be . . .' began Hamlet, *'that is the question.'*

But the moment was lost. William Tell had triumphed.

'I am *so* sorry,' said Matt, slowly. 'I can't believe that actually happened. It was bloody Beano! I am so embarrassed.'

They were descending the steps and leaving the theatre.

'It doesn't matter,' lied Laura. 'These things happen. It's probably not the first time and I'm sure it won't be the last.'

'I wouldn't mind, but there are notices on every door asking people to turn off their mobiles before entering. I forgot I even had it with me.'

'Don't worry about it,' said Laura. 'The couple next to us were killing themselves laughing. I think you made their evening! Anyway, they probably have mobile phones in modern day Palestine!'

Matt wasn't *too* familiar with the night spots of Manchester but Beano had recommended a couple of bars. They talked as they walked and conversation was relaxed and easy.

'What did you think of the performance?' asked Laura.

'To be honest, it wasn't really my type of thing,' admitted Matt. 'I've never really been into Shakespeare and modern day Shakespeare's even more confusing. It didn't seem right, all that old English flowery language in present day Palestine.'

'I know what you're saying,' agreed Laura. 'I prefer my Shakespeare straight, but the acting was brilliant. Surely you agree that the acting was brilliant?'

'I had to study *A Midsummer Night's Dream* at school,' continued Matt, completely ignoring Laura's comment. 'I hated it! Shakespeare was a weird geek, if you ask me. Let's face it, only a weird geek would write about fairies and elves and things.'

Laura laughed. 'Do you realise,' she said, 'you've just summed up the greatest playwright ever as "a weird geek"! I shouldn't bother with a career in literary criticism, Matt!'

They eventually found the area, bursting with late night life and noise. Matt acted as if it was a natural setting for him. Beano had given him the names of three bars to look out for and, spotting Victoria's, Matt said, 'It's OK in here, Laura. You'll like it. Let's get a drink, should we?'

Laura looked a bit surprised but she followed him through the door.

There was a good atmosphere inside the bar. The music was loud and the place was absolutely packed. They were queuing four deep at the bar.

'What would you like to drink?' asked Matt. 'It might take a while.'

'I'll have a Bacardi Breezer,' said Laura. 'Any flavour will do. I'll just go to the Ladies. See you in a couple of minutes.'

Matt took his place at the back of the pack and edged slowly towards the bar. It was staffed by four young men, all wearing the same navy blue vests. They were fascinating to watch as they juggled the glasses and bottles and engaged in a stream of constant banter with the drinkers.

'Paul's my favourite,' said a youth with

died blonde hair clutching an empty glass next to Matt. 'Lovely mover, if you know what I mean.'

'Yes, he's very good,' agreed Matt. 'They're all very good!'

'Are you on your own?' enquired the youth.

'No, no – I'm with my girlfriend,' said Matt, feeling a surge of pride.

'Oh, I see,' said the youth, sounding disappointed, and he turned to chat to someone else.

Matt reached the bar and the 'lovely mover' served him.

'What can I get you, mate? What's your fancy?'

'Two Bacardi Breezers, please – different flavours – and a pint of John Smith's.'

'Two in a bed and a big one to go with them!' announced Paul, and he juggled the bottles in the air before whipping their tops off!

Laura was waiting for him over by one of the games machines. She smiled as he approached and she took the two Bacardi Breezers from him, putting one on top of the Quizmaster and taking a gulp from the lime flavour. 'You're a bitter drinker, then?' she said, nodding towards Matt's pint.

'I think I'm one of the few that is,' replied Matt, looking around. He almost had to shout to make himself heard. 'Even the blokes are drinking mixers.'

And then he froze, suddenly, and stared past Laura's left shoulder.

'Matt, what's the matter?' she said, glancing round. 'Is there someone you know?'

Matt leaned forward and raised his hand to his mouth in a gesture of discretion. 'Don't stare,' he said, 'but there's two fellas behind you with their arms around each other!'

Laura laughed. 'I know,' she said, 'look over there.'

Matt followed her gaze to a secluded table in the far corner. The area was dimly lit. At first, he saw two couples and they were perched on each other's knees, flirting with each other. And then he realised with horror that they were all men. He took a step forward and stared, as if to confirm that his eyes weren't playing tricks on him.

'It's a gay bar,' said Laura, putting a reassuring hand on his shoulder. 'Anyone can see it's a gay bar, Matt! It's not a problem for you, is it?'

Matt put his glass down on the nearest table. He removed Laura's Bacardi Breezer from her hand and placed it next to his pint.

'Come on,' he said, placing a firm hand on her arm and edging her towards the door. 'We're out of here!'

'I'll kill him!' said Matt, as the taxi made its way

back along Wilmslow Road. 'I am actually going to physically kill him! That was Beano's idea of a joke!'

Laura couldn't stop laughing. 'You should have seen your face! It was brilliant! I haven't enjoyed myself so much for years!'

She rested her head on his shoulder and he slipped his arm around her.

'We could still have a drink,' he said hesitantly, 'back at my place, if you want?'

'Why not,' said Laura, 'that sounds a good idea to me. After all, it is the weekend.'

Chapter 8

There was no way Linton was going to keep away from Chorlton. He respected his father, he was a good man, but he didn't respect him enough to keep away from Marsha and she was his reason for going to Chorlton. She hung around there on the streets with her friends. Marsha was a year younger than Linton but she looked much older and she was certainly more streetwise. Marsha was tall and slim; she wore tight jeans and her hair was swept back from her forehead and brightly braided. Her deep brown eyes were wide and inviting and there was no way Linton could resist the call.

It was a few days after Linton had been beaten up at the bus station. It was only seven-thirty in the evening but a white frost had already formed and Linton could see his breath as he walked. Before leaving home, Linton had promised his father that he would be back in by ten o'clock but he had no intention of keeping his promise. He strolled up to the group of kids at the corner of Chorlton Green, hands in pockets, hooded top pulled up. A couple of the kids were smoking cigarettes, cans of lager on the wall besides them. Marsha took a swig from a bottle of cider as he approached.

'What happened to you, man? Your face looks a mess!'

It was Rufus who spoke and when Rufus spoke everyone listened.

'It's nothing,' said Linton, knowing full well what the reaction would be. 'A bit of trouble with some white kids on the way home the other night. I'm OK, Rufus.'

'Trouble with some white kids?' repeated Rufus. 'It's not acceptable, man. Tell me what happened?'

'It was at the bus station,' explained Linton. He was beginning to enjoy being the centre of attention. 'They came round the corner and they were too quick for me. I should have reacted faster.'

Marsha stepped forward and placed a soft hand onto his bruised mouth. He felt a surge of excitement. 'Who were they?' she said, and he was so close that he could smell the sweet cider on her breath. 'Did you recognise them?'

'I've never seen them before,' said Linton. 'Probably students. They'd been drinking. One of them could hardly walk.'

'It's not acceptable,' repeated Rufus, and

he flicked his cigarette end onto the pavement and ground it with his boot. 'We should do something about it.'

'Forget it,' said Linton. 'I told you I'm all right.'

Rufus took a step forward and stared straight into Linton's eyes. 'We look after our own, man. We can't let this sort of thing happen to one of our own. Do you understand what I'm saying?'

'Rufus is right,' said Marsha. 'We have to look after each other.'

Linton was beginning to feel uncomfortable. He shuffled from one foot to the other. He was aware that his ribs were still hurting.

'I know where they hang out, man.'

The new voice belonged to Ricky. Linton didn't trust him. To use his father's words, he was trouble.

'Them students, I mean. They drink in the pub opposite the university in Didsbury. I say we should pay them a visit.'

'But we don't know who they are,' protested Linton. 'I don't know if I'd recognise them again.'

'It don't matter who they are,' said Rufus. He was still staring straight into Linton's eyes. 'Students are students. I'm with Ricky; we should pay them a visit. What do you say, Linton? Are you with us or not?'

Linton said nothing for a moment. A couple more years and he would be a student himself. He knew his father expected it of him.

'Answer me, man!' persisted Rufus. 'Are you with us or not?'

'I'm with you,' said Linton, nodding his head. 'Count me in.'

'That's good,' said Rufus, and he glanced round at the others. 'Now let's make some arrangements.'

Chapter 9

It was the last week in November. The clock showed 6.45 a.m. and Matt was awake. The room was dark and he lay on his side, quite still, staring at Laura who was still asleep next to him. She had stayed quite a bit since the night of the theatre visit. Matt had felt awkward asking her a second time. What if she didn't want to get that involved? In the end, he dropped it in almost casually, while they were having a drink one evening in The Old Cock.

'Why don't you stay over at my place tonight? Save you from putting up with all those noises from Dina?'

He was surprised how quickly she had agreed.

'OK,' she had said, as if he had asked her if she wanted another drink. 'But I have to tell you – you won't like me in the morning. I'm awful in the morning.'

Matt loved her in the morning. She was soft and warm and vulnerable and when she woke up she stretched like a kitten. He had forgotten just how good it felt to wake up next to someone.

This particular morning, the alarm went off at seven o'clock and, sure enough, Laura stretched and sighed and rolled over with her eyes still closed. He could feel her warm, sleepy breath on his face and he just stared at her for a few moments.

'Morning,' said Matt, eventually, and he kissed her on the forehead.

'Morning,' she muttered in reply. 'What time is it?' She still hadn't opened her eyes.

'Same as usual,' said Matt. 'You always ask that. It's seven o'clock, the same as it always is when the alarm goes off.'

'I was hoping the alarm had got it wrong,' said Laura, and she pulled the covers over her head.

Breakfast was simple; tea and toast taken perched on two stools in the kitchen. Matt didn't usually bother with breakfast when he was on his own – he was usually too late – but Laura insisted that she couldn't go to work on an empty stomach, so it was always tea and toast when she stayed with him.

'I won't see you tonight,' said Laura, stuffing a set of exercise books into a plastic carrier bag. 'It's Parents' Evening. I'll go straight back to the flat after that.'

'OK,' said Matt. 'Tomorrow, then. I'll give

you a ring after work tomorrow.'

'Fine,' said Laura. 'Have a good day!' And she was gone, stepping over the growing pile of free newspapers in the hallway, wrenching open the front door, leaving Matt to listen to the morning babble on the kitchen radio.

'So how come I'm honoured?' asked Beano. He had just wiped some froth from his mouth with the end of his sleeve. 'Has she done the sensible thing and dumped you?'

They were sitting at their favourite table in The Old Cock.

'Of course she hasn't,' said Matt. 'She knows when she's on to a good thing. As a matter of fact, it's Parents' Evening. She's going back to the flat afterwards.'

'Do you know you've gone really smug since you've met that girl. You walk around with a permanent stupid grin on your face.'

'It's called contentment, Beano. You wouldn't know the feeling.'

'It's called getting your oats, you lucky sod. Are you making up for lost time, or something?'

'You want to try it yourself, Beano. It's very good for you, especially if you've got a bad back.'

'The only thing I'm getting is old,' said

Beano, and he took a prolonged gulp of his pint before wiping his mouth again.

The pub was fairly crowded, as usual. Matt recognised a few of the faces. The blonde girl and the lecturer were in, sitting next to each other in the opposite corner, he with his hand on her knee. The student who had downed the pint of lager was also there, sitting with a noisy group who roared with laughter at regular intervals. A group of older men in their late twenties or early thirties, about six in all, sat around a large, rectangular table. They looked different from the rest of the crowd, well-dressed in suits and collars and ties, drinking gin and tonic and speaking in loud voices. One of them had a laptop computer and he kept tapping in information and then explaining the outcome to his colleagues.

Beano didn't like them. They looked too successful.

'It's all show,' he announced, scowling. 'Do they really have to sit around a computer in a pub? It's pathetic!'

'That's the "New Didsbury" for you,' said Matt. 'Mobile phones and laptop computers. You wouldn't have seen people like them in here ten years ago.'

'I'll get us another pint in,' said Beano, reaching for Matt's glass. 'Unless you'd prefer a gin and tonic, that is.'

Beano made his way to the bar leaving

Matt to do some more people watching. It was fascinating. He stared hard at the 'New Didsbury' group and he was sure he recognised one of them. He was a well-built chap with heavily gelled jet-black hair. Matt couldn't quite place him but he was certain he knew him. He was the only one of the group who was drinking a pint and, as Matt watched, he pulled out a pack of cigarettes and flicked the top open. He took a cigarette out and tapped it on the table. It all looked so familiar. One of the others made a comment and pointed at the *No Smoking* sign. That was one thing that had changed since Matt was a student. The Old Cock had always been filled with a haze of smoke but the no smoking ban had put a stop to that. The guy Matt recognised laughed out loud, too loud, before returning the cigarette to its packet. Matt even recognised the laugh, a false laugh designed to humour his friend. He knew him; Matt was sure he knew him.

And then Matt remembered. He knew him from his time at university. It was Lewis – Lewis Jordan. His hair had been much longer ten years ago and had hung over his face like a pair of curtains. The smart suit had replaced the student uniform of faded denims and oversized jumper but it was definitely Lewis Jordan.

Matt had never liked him. He had studied P.E. and had represented the county at rugby. Matt remembered the rugby crowd dominating half of the college bar, especially on a Friday night, with their stupid drinking songs and boorish behaviour. Most of them had been an ugly lot with flat noses and big ears. He couldn't understand why so many of the girls found them attractive.

Beano had put him right on that one. 'It's bloody obvious!' he explained. 'Look at the size of them! There's only one thing they're after, isn't there!'

Lewis had been different from the others; strong and handsome and very self-confident.

Matt was, of course, jealous. But he wasn't jealous now as he looked at Lewis with his slicked-back hair and his smarmy laugh. If that's what he had turned into, he wasn't at all jealous now.

Beano had been a long time getting the pints. Matt glanced across to the bar and realised why. He was leaning against the bar, two full pints in front of him, talking to a red-haired young woman. There was no mistaking that streaked red hair and array of steel earrings – it was Dina.

'Incredible!' said Matt, out loud. 'Can't take my eyes off him for five minutes!'

Matt looked across to the Canal Bar, where Meg was sitting on her own, eating crisps and looking miserable.

Beano gave a few parting comments that made Dina laugh and then he carried the pints across to Matt.

'You want to watch that one,' said Matt, seriously. 'I could tell you things about her that would make your toes curl.'

'Really?' said Beano. He looked interested. 'Tell me more.'

'Another time, maybe,' said Matt. 'Have a look over there.' He nodded towards the New Didsbury group. 'Do you recognise anyone? The one with the Dracula hairstyle?'

'Bloody hell!' said Beano. 'It's Lewis Jordan! Curtains!'

'Changed a bit, hasn't he?' said Matt. 'Obviously moved up in the world.'

'He still looks a prat,' said Beano, supping his pint. 'A well-dressed prat, I grant you.'

'I wonder what he does for a living?' said Matt. 'Makes a lot of money by the look of him. I wonder what they all do?'

'Who cares,' said Beano. 'If making money means you've got to look like that lot, I'll give it a miss.'

'Still,' said Matt, thoughtfully, 'it would be interesting to know what he does.'

It was eleven-thirty by the time Matt arrived home. The day's usual grey cloud cover had given way to clear skies and a glistening frost had already formed on the pavement and the parked cars. Matt shivered as he turned the key in his lock. The front door was sticking worse than ever and he had to push against it to force it open. He made a mental note to phone a joiner the very next day.

The house was cold. He had central heating but the timer had switched it off half an hour ago. It wasn't that efficient, anyway. Matt went straight to the kitchen and flicked the switch on the kettle. He knew it was bad to drink coffee last thing at night but with no Laura to warm him up it seemed like a good idea.

Matt carried his mug into the living room and noticed the red button flashing on his answer machine. There was one message displayed and Matt knew straight away that it would be Laura. She had probably rung him after Parents' Evening. Perhaps she had changed her mind and wanted to come round after all. He hadn't mentioned that he was going to the pub with Beano.

Matt sat down in the chair next to the phone and pressed play. He cupped the warm mug in his hands and waited for Laura's voice.

'Matthew – it's Mum. I've got some bad news, I'm afraid.' The voice was strained with emotion. 'It's your father. He's been taken ill. He's in hospital. They think he's had a stroke.'

Chapter 10

Matt leaned forward on the black iron rail that ran the length of Whitby harbour and tucked in to his steaming hot parcel of fish and chips. It had taken him just over two and a half hours to drive to Whitby, the town where he had lived for the first eighteen years of his life, before going to university; the town where his mother and father still lived, in the same fisherman's cottage they had inhabited for thirty-five years, ever since they were married.

It had been an early start that morning. A few clothes and toiletries stuffed into an overnight bag and on the road by seven o'clock. Matt had stopped briefly at the Hartshead Moor services to make a phone call to the office. The answer phone was on and he left a garbled message of explanation. He had made a quick phone call to Laura the previous night and he had decided he would speak to her again later when he had more time and more definite news. Still, he felt a touch guilty that it was Laura on his mind and not his father as he continued his journey up past

York and over the bleak, desolate moors towards Whitby.

Matt had parked at the railway station, just across the road from the quayside. It was where he always parked when he returned home to Whitby. There was no facility to park outside the cottage in the narrow street, still cobbled to preserve tradition and to please the tourists. Matt would park at the station and walk the short distance to Henrietta Street, past the one hundred and ninety-nine steps that led up to St Mary's Church and the ruins of Whitby Abbey, but before he returned home, he would steal some time for himself. And so, there he was, leaning over the rail staring at the fishing boats and the piles of crab cages, eating morning fresh fish and chips straight from the paper. But this time it was different. This time his father was ill in hospital.

Matt had never known his father to be ill. All those years he had gone out on the fishing boat, day after day, even when the weather was so bad that others remained in harbour, his father had never had so much as a cold. He had seemed indestructible but now he was lying in a hospital bed and Matt didn't know how he was going to cope.

He smiled to himself as he pictured his father leaving the cottage for work, almost smothered in his fisherman's clothes, his great boots and his dark green woolly hat. Matt closed his eyes and listened to the incessant sound of the seagulls overhead. He could see himself as a child, watching from his attic bedroom window as his father left for work. In his head, he could hear his father's gruff voice shouting goodbye. He could picture his father taking a few paces down the cobbled street and then turning and waving up at the window before disappearing down one of the side alleyways that led steeply down to the fishing boats.

And then he would return, hours later, wet and cold and smelling of fish and the sea, and Matt's mother would sigh with relief that he had arrived home safely. They lived with that unspoken fear, that awful dread that one day he would not return. It was worse when the weather was stormy, as it was more often than not on that exposed east coast. The vicious wind would howl in from the North Sea, causing huge waves to crash through the harbour entrance and pound against the nearby cliffs. Matt would go up to his room, from where he could see over the tops of the cottages opposite. He would stare out into the harbour, into the grey, lashing rain and he would imagine what it was like to be at the mercy of the sea and the storm and he vowed that when he grew up he wouldn't put his life at risk, as his father did, week in, week out.

He had never forgotten the terrible day that

the *May Ellen* went down. He still kept a copy of the *Whitby Gazette* that had reported the tragedy on the front page. Nineteen years had passed but that November day still haunted him.

The storm had blown up so quickly, so unexpectedly. It was mid-afternoon but it was as dark as night. Matt watched from his attic window as his father appeared from the alleyway, striding anxiously over the soaked cobbles towards the cottage. He listened from the top of the stairs as his father explained to his mother that the *May Ellen* was late in. He heard him say in an anxious, faltering voice, 'There's something wrong, Anna. She should be back by now.' And then Auntie Sarah from next door came into the cottage with young Emily. They were in the living room with Matt's mother and father and Auntie Sarah and Emily were crying, and Matt didn't understand why. He crept out of his room and sat at the top of the stairs and he listened to them both crying, the waves crashing and the wind howling in sympathy. It was the following morning that his mother told him the *May Ellen* hadn't come back and that Emily's father was missing but it was only when they went to school and Mr Hill, the Headteacher, announced in assembly that the boat was lost that he realised Emily's father was dead. Emily's father was dead and she would never,

ever see him again.

There was a sudden whooshing sound and a loud crack in the sky and it shook Matt out of his memories. The first flare was followed by a second and Matt saw the trail of smoke before it exploded and echoed across the harbour. He was used to the flares. They were tested regularly. The lifeboat remained in harbour but Matt was stirred into action.

He scrunched up his paper and threw the scraps of his fish and chips into a nearby bin before walking the short distance to Henrietta Street. It had changed over the last twenty years. Most of the buildings were now let as holiday cottages, the original residents having made a healthy profit. Old Jacob still lived at Number 9. It was the one cottage in the whole street that was run down and in need of repair. The paint was flaking from the door and the front windows and water poured from the gutters every time it rained. A tattered grey curtain hung limply across the front window to prevent the tourists from peering into the cottage. There was no way Old Jacob was going to leave his lifelong home, despite several good offers from different developers. Auntie Sarah had moved into a flat on the outskirts of Whitby when Emily had married but Matt's parents had held on to Number 4.

Matt stood on the pavement outside the cottage and stared at the blue door. He didn't want to see his mother; he didn't know what to say. He could feel his heart beating faster as he pressed the bell. And then his mother was there, in front of him, standing in the open doorway. He stepped forward and she threw her arms around him.

Matt's mum had always made a good cup of tea. They sat there, the two of them, in the living room, cradling the dark blue mugs in their hands. She had stopped crying and she was talking quietly; a sentence, and then a pause and then another sentence.

'He was just watching television, as he did every other evening when he got back from the pub. I knew he wasn't right. He kept holding his shoulder and rubbing his arm.'

She sipped the strong, hot liquid and wiped her eyes with a small, triangular handkerchief.

'I asked him about it – but you know what he's like. He told me to stop fussing. The next thing I knew, he'd slumped forward in his chair. He didn't make a sound – he just slumped forward.'

She raised a thin, trembling hand to her head and pushed her fingers through her hair. Matt was surprised how much older she looked. He had never thought of his mother as old but now, suddenly, she looked tired and strained, as if all those years of worry had finally caught up with her.

'I didn't know what to do. I went across and I shook him. I kept saying his name. I couldn't understand what was happening. Isn't that awful, Matthew? I didn't know what to do!'

'It's all right, Mum. You did the right thing. You got him into hospital.'

'But I wasted time, Matt. It was minutes before I called the ambulance. I just knelt down by his chair. What if I caused him more damage?'

'You can't think like that, Mum. You got him into hospital and the doctors have told you he's already responding. Thousands of people make good recoveries from strokes these days. It's no big deal.'

'He doesn't get enough exercise since he's retired. It used to keep him strong going out on the fishing boat. It was hard work but it was keeping him fit. There wasn't an ounce of fat on him. Only last week I told him he was getting podgy. It's the drink that does it, you know – not my cooking. He goes down to The George every other night. It's not good for him, not without exercise.'

'He's gone down to The George for years,' Matt reminded her. 'Ever since I can remember. And he's smoked like a chimney for years. Things have just caught up with him, that's all.'

'Well, things will have to change when he gets better. No cigarettes, less beer and more walking. That's one thing about Whitby – there's plenty of walking to be had.'

'He won't like it,' said Matt, trying to picture his dad going for gentle walks along the coast. 'I can tell you now – he will not like it!'

Matt finished his drink and then took his bag up to his attic bedroom. That was the comforting thing about returning to Whitby – nothing ever changed. His room was just as he had left it when he was eighteen. There was the *Star Wars* quilt cover on his bed and his Leeds United posters were still on the walls, a bit yellow and faded but still in place. Matt had never really been interested in football but the other boys at school had been mad keen on Leeds United and Matt had done his best to join in.

He put his bag down on the wicker chair that had always stood in the corner of his bedroom and he stared out of the window. His mother had opened it to let in some fresh air and he closed his eyes and breathed in deeply. He opened them again and there was the view, over the rooftops to the harbour. The only thing missing was the sight of his father, waving up at him as he returned home from work, windswept, tired and hungry.

Matt's dad was in a side room off the main ward. The two of them, Matt and his mum, stood at the window and stared in before they entered. He was asleep. Or at least, he had his eyes closed.

Matt was surprised to see that he didn't look that different. If anything, his mother looked worse. She was trembling by his side and Matt placed his arm around her shoulder to comfort her. His father's weather-beaten face, aged with years of sea and salt, stood out against the white pillows, his shock of grey-white hair looking straggled and untidy and he desperately needed a shave.

'Let's go inside,' said his mother, lifting a hand to remove Matt's arm. 'He'll want to see you.'

His eyes opened as they approached the bed. He didn't recognise them for a moment. He stared at Matt and then glanced towards his wife, as if to ask for help.

'Hello, Jack. How are you, love?' She leaned over him and kissed his forehead. 'Our Matt's come to see you. It's what you've been waiting for.'

He turned his gaze back towards his son and his eyes widened in sudden recognition.

'Hello, Dad. What have you been up to, then? Causing everyone trouble, eh?' It wasn't a good thing to say. Why could he never find the right words?

'Matthew – it's good to see you. Thanks for coming.'

The voice was slightly slurred but the words were clear enough. Matt had feared much worse.

'I came as soon as I heard, Dad. You didn't think I'd ignore you, did you?'

Matt's mum pulled up a couple of chairs and they sat close to the bed.

'Your mum said you'd come. She said you'd be worried.'

He was having difficulty turning his head and he gave up after a few attempts and stared at the ceiling.

'How are you feeling?' asked Matt. 'What have they said to you?'

'I've had a stroke. You know I've had a stroke, don't you?'

'I know,' said Matt, quietly. 'Mum told me it was a stroke.'

'It's funny – I thought only old 'uns had strokes. I never thought of myself as old – until this.'

A young nurse breezed into the room, smiled at the visitors and then looked at the chart at the bottom of his bed. 'Are you all right, Mr Hudson? Fighting fit yet?'

Matt thought he saw his dad try to smile. He decided to answer for him.

'You won't be able to keep this one in bed. He'll be driving you all mad soon. You'll be glad to get rid of him!'

The young nurse smiled and winked at Matt. 'Oh, don't you worry. We'll handle him. He'll do as he's told while he's in here!' She adjusted his pillows and poured out a fresh glass of water. Matt couldn't help but notice how attractive she looked and he felt a pang of guilt as she left the room.

'It's me left side, mostly. I can't feel me left leg. It's coming back a bit in me arm but I can't move me left leg.'

'Don't worry, Jack. It's early days yet. It's only been a few hours. The doctor told you it would take time.' Matt's mum was struggling to keep back the tears. Her voice betrayed her feelings.

'I know that, Anna,' sighed her husband. 'I know that. But I won't be a good patient, will I? I'm never ill.'

'Well, you are now,' said Matt's mum, more firmly. 'And you'll have to do as you're told, for a change, just as the nurse said.'

Matt didn't know what to say. He felt awkward. 'It's a good job you're right handed,' he observed.

God! He'd done it again! He could have crawled under the bed with the bed pan!

Chapter 11

Laura was late for her appointment. She had arranged to view the flat at six-fifteen and it was already twenty minutes to seven. She banged the door shut on her Citroën and clicked the remote to lock it. East Didsbury might be a desirable area but that only made it more of a target for car crime. She had managed to park right outside Grange Court and she stood for a moment, looking up at the large, three-storey building, each flat with its own separate balcony. She liked what she saw. Grange Road itself was wide and open with plenty of parking, giving an impression of spaciousness. That's what Laura needed more than anything – her own space. The price was right, too, not overly expensive for Didsbury, even if it was only a one bedroom flat. She could cope with the repayments. She was earning a decent wage and she'd managed to put some money to one side for a deposit.

A car door clicked closed behind her and a voice enquired: 'Miss Williams?' Laura glanced round to see a smart young man dressed in a grey suit, his hand outstretched to greet her. Again, she liked what she saw and she returned his smile as she accepted the firm handshake.

'Sorry I'm late,' she said. 'I was held up at work.'

'No problem. I was a few minutes late myself. I'm Lewis Jordan, by the way.' He produced a card by way of identification. 'We spoke on the phone.'

'Pleased to meet you, Mr Jordan. Can we have a look at the flat?'

They walked up the short driveway to the main entrance. A security light came on as they approached and Laura noticed a parking area for the residents over to the right. There were not many spaces but Didsbury was terrible for parking and anything would help. Lewis Jordan pulled a bunch of keys from his pocket, each one carefully labelled, and he opened the front door, standing to one side for Laura to go before him.

'There's an intercom system linked to each individual flat,' he explained, slipping effortlessly into estate-agent-speak. 'Excellent for security. It gives tenants complete peace of mind.'

He was so confident. Laura smiled politely and followed him up the wide stairs. She thought the plain white entrance area was a bit unwelcoming and there was definitely a musty smell but she said nothing.

'As you know, Number 21 is a first floor

apartment to the rear of the building,' continued Lewis. He had stopped outside a wooden veneered door and was fiddling with the keys again. He found the right one and inserted it into the lock. Once inside he flicked on the light and said, 'I think you'll be impressed. We have no problem selling flats in this area.'

Laura stepped into the small hallway and on through into the main room. It was bigger than she had imagined, tastefully furnished with minimum fuss. A beige three-piece suite; a small drop leaf table; a modern standard lamp and a few pictures. There was an oblong coffee table next to the large bay window and Laura walked across and stared out into the darkness.

'You're not really overlooked at the back,' said Lewis. 'You look out onto Didsbury Park – if you can see past the trees, that is. You can also see the parking area to your right, which is quite handy.'

'It's OK,' said Laura, looking around. She loved it immediately but she didn't wish to sound too enthusiastic. 'What about the kitchen and the bedroom?'

Lewis took her through to the kitchen – small but well equipped with all that she would need to look after herself. She opened the oven door and then peered into the fridge. Both were clean. There was no way this had been a student flat.

The bedroom was fine. A single bed was pushed against one wall and a freestanding white wardrobe with a matching set of drawers stood opposite. The view from the bedroom window was also over Didsbury Park.

'It's a bit small; the bedroom, I mean. I like the flat but the bedroom's a bit small.'

'It's only to sleep in,' explained Lewis. 'It's not as if you'd spend a lot of time in here. What else would you want to do in the bedroom?'

Laura blushed slightly and she was certain that it had been noticed. 'I'll have to think about it,' she said. She moved out of the bedroom and back into the lounge. 'Do you think the owner would drop the price a bit? If I made an offer, I mean?'

Lewis scratched his chin and looked doubtful. 'I'm not sure about that,' he said. 'It comes fully furnished, don't forget. Everything you see is included in the price. I can try him, if you like but I do have someone else coming to view on Friday. I tell you what – why don't we discuss it over a drink? There's a little Italian wine bar in the village that would be perfect.'

Laura was taken aback. The suggestion had come from nowhere, out of the blue. To her surprise, she found herself saying, 'Yes – thanks. Why not? I'd like that.' And for some reason she felt guilty.

Lewis moved forward and placed his hand

on Laura's arm to guide her out of the flat. He flicked off the light and pulled the door closed behind him. Perfect. Things were looking up in the estate agent business.

As they shared a bottle of Chianti, Laura's guilt increased and she suddenly realised why. He had taken her to the same Italian Bar she had been to with Matt. The conversation was even the same. There she was explaining about her job and the house in Chorlton and how she needed more space. She even found herself repeating the details of Dina's sex life.

Lewis was so different to Matt. She couldn't help but compare them. For a start, he was better looking, there was no doubt about that, and although Matt made her laugh, Lewis was more interesting. Even Laura realised that Matt had a boring job with little prospect of advancement, but Lewis – he was different.

'It's great,' he explained, 'I've been with the firm for five years now and the way things are going I'll be breaking away and starting my own business soon. The house market's been up and down over recent year's but there always seems to be a good turnover in an area like Didsbury. There's a lot of money to be made in this game, I can tell you.'

'Yes, but estate agents aren't exactly well

thought of in society, are they?' said Lisa. 'Let's face it, they're only one rung up the ladder from the taxman!'

'I don't give a damn what anyone thinks of me,' said Lewis, pouring himself another glass of wine. 'I've bought my own property, I'm driving the car I want and I've got a load of spare cash in my pocket. What more could a man want?'

'A relationship?' suggested Laura. She refused Lewis' offer of another glass of wine, remembering that she had to drive back to Chorlton. Instead, he topped up his own glass. 'Is there some lucky woman in your life?'

'I'm between relationships,' he said. 'I don't really want to get into anything heavy at the moment – I'm having too much of a good time. As soon as things start to get heavy I back off pretty quickly. What about you?'

She paused for a moment and then she said, 'The same. I'm between relationships. I've no intention of getting too involved just yet. As I told you, I need some time to myself.'

There was that pang of guilt again – but she realised that she meant what she said.

'That's why I'm looking for a place of my own,' she continued. 'No commitments and no complications.'

'So what do you think of the flat?' said Lewis. 'Have I got a sale or not?'

She was beginning to enjoy herself. 'I

just need a little bit of time to think it over,' she said. 'Why don't we meet here again tomorrow evening? You never know, I might have a decision for you by then!'

Chapter 12

Matt arrived home just before eight o'clock. It normally took him about two and a half hours from Whitby but the journey across The Pennines had been particularly difficult. The weather had closed in, with driving sleet limiting visibility and reducing the traffic to a crawl. How many times had that happened? Matt hated that section of the motorway across the top of The Pennines. Even on a good day the landscape was barren and bleak, brown scrubland with little sign of life. Matt shivered every time he drove past Saddleworth Moor, with its dark, secret past. It was always a relief to descend towards the Lancashire mill towns.

He had tried to ring Laura a few times without any luck. He had, of course, spoken to her on the night he'd heard the news about his father. He had rung late, having had a black coffee to steady his nerves and he'd got her out of bed, shattered after her Parents' Evening. He had explained about his father and told her that he would be away for a few days, and she had muttered how sorry she was in a sleepy voice and asked him to keep in touch, before crawling back into bed.

But he had not spoken to her since. He rang on his first evening away, after he had visited the hospital, and Dina had explained that she was out viewing a flat in Didsbury. Matt recalled her telling him something about a new flat and he had agreed that it was a good idea. He had lied. If he was honest, he couldn't see the point. He couldn't understand why she did not just move in with him and save herself some money. They seemed to get on so well together that it was inevitable, eventually.

He had called again that very lunchtime. He'd rung her on her mobile before at lunchtime and she had always answered. He was a bit surprised when, after several rings, the phone went completely dead. Maybe she was in a meeting or something.

Matt decided that the best course of action was just to turn up at Laura's house in Chorlton. They could go out for a drink to one of the local pubs. He didn't like the Chorlton pubs as much as The Old Cock but he had a lot to tell her and he couldn't wait to see her.

By eight-thirty he was outside the large stone house in Chorlton that Laura shared with the other two girls. There was a dim glow in an upstairs room that Matt knew to be Dina's bedroom. Everywhere else was in darkness. Matt shivered as he stood on the doorstep. He pressed the bell and waited for a response. Nothing. He tried again, and he pulled up the collar on his jacket as he waited in the heavy drizzle. There was still no reply.

Matt had a key. Laura had given it to him just a few days before he had been called to Whitby. He hadn't wanted to take it at first, until Laura told him that Dina had given a key to half the men in Chorlton. For some reason, that seemed to make him feel better, and now, as he stood in the cold rain, he was glad that he had accepted it.

Matt opened the door and stepped inside. The hallway was dark and he wasn't sure where to find the light switch. He fumbled his way along the wall until he came to a door that led into the lounge. Pushing it open, Matt entered. A thin light found its way through the window from a nearby street lamp. Matt reached for the light switch and flicked it on.

The room was in a terrible mess. There was an oblong coffee table cluttered with unwashed mugs and used plates; there was a brown ashtray, obviously acquired from one of the local pubs, overflowing with cigarette stubs, nestled in amongst the plates. The smell of smoke and stale ash lingered in the air. Various beer bottles were scattered over the floor and a half eaten piece of pizza adorned the couch. It wasn't even on a plate; it just seemed to be stuck there. The room was littered with newspapers and magazines – everything from *The Guardian* to *The Big Issue*. Matt suddenly understood why Laura needed a place of her own. He had been in the house before but it hadn't been that bad.

Matt's eyes were drawn towards a white, plastic washing maiden which stood in front of the central heating radiator. It was full of underwear – bras, panties, thongs, suspenders – the lot. There were at least four different sets in colours that ranged from glossy black to bright red.

'That's not Laura's,' said Matt, out loud. 'It's got to be Dina's. Bloody hell!'

Matt was about to look for some paper to leave Laura a note when a distinctive voice called from an upstairs room.

'Meg! . . . Is that you? Come up for a minute will you, Meg!'

He jumped, at first, startled to realise that someone was home. It was Dina. He knew it was Dina and he suddenly felt embarrassed that he had been looking at her underwear.

Matt didn't know what to do. He moved to the bottom of the stairs and shouted, 'It's me, Dina! Matt! I've just got back from Whitby! I was hoping to find Laura at home!'

There was no response for a moment, as if Dina was trying to come to terms with this unexpected voice. And then Dina made up her mind:

'Matt! Come on up, will you! Front bedroom – just come straight in!'

Matt knew which room was Dina's. Laura had told him she'd grabbed the best bedroom as soon as they had moved into the house. He climbed the stairs, pushed open the bedroom door and froze to the spot in immediate shock.

Dina was stretched out on the bed absolutely stark naked. Her arms were raised above and behind her head and her wrists were handcuffed to the metal bed frame. Matt couldn't believe his eyes. Diffused blue light from a small table lamp added to the surrealism of the scene. He stood and stared, with his mouth half open, and Dina stared back at him. The moment seemed frozen in time.

'Unusual, I know,' said Dina, trying to force a thin smile. 'I've had a bit of boyfriend trouble – an argument – he left me . . . in this state.'

Matt couldn't speak. He put one hand on the door handle to steady himself. Ridiculously, he found himself staring at her red hair, which had clearly been freshly treated. He lowered his eyes slowly and was shocked to see another streak of red hair. He couldn't believe it. He grabbed the door handle tighter.

'I don't suppose you could release me, could you?'

Dina's voice brought him round. He shook his head and said, in a hoarse whisper, 'Where's the key?'

'It's over there.' She nodded towards a small round table, and he noticed the metal key next to the lamp. 'Bastard put it there deliberately so that I could see it but couldn't reach it.'

Matt moved into the room and picked up the key. It was as if it was happening to someone else. He approached the bed and, taking hold of Dina's right wrist, he released the handcuff. Her arm dropped immediately and she shook her hand to bring back the circulation. Matt moved round the bed and clicked open the other handcuff.

'I can't tell you how good that feels,' said Dina, sitting upright and crossing her legs. 'Thanks, Matt!'

'I'll . . . er . . . just wait downstairs,' said Matt, backing out of the room, 'while you get some clothes on.'

Chapter 13

Dina put down Matt's mug of coffee in the one remaining space on the coffee table. It was strong and black and just what he needed. It was only when he took a sip that he realised how bad it was.

'I'm really, really sorry,' said Dina. 'I don't make a habit of that sort of thing, you know.'

Matt knew different. He didn't say anything. Instead, he glanced across to the washing maiden but averted his eyes quickly.

'Laura told me about your father.' Dina swept a pile of papers from an armchair onto the floor and she sat down. 'I was sorry to hear the news. How is he?'

'There's some improvement,' said Matt. 'It's going to be a long job and we're not sure how it will leave him. He won't be the easiest of patients.'

'My grandfather died from a stroke,' said Dina, trying to be helpful, and they both stared into their coffee mugs. 'It's frightening,' she continued, 'makes you realise that you've got to get the most out of life while you can.'

There was no doubt in Matt's mind that Dina got the most out of life.

'I was hoping to see Laura,' said Matt, changing the subject. 'Has she got a meeting, or something?'

'Yes – sort of,' said Dina. Matt sensed that she was uncomfortable. 'Not at school, though. Something to do with the new flat she's after.'

'What, at this time of night? That's a bit odd, isn't it?'

'Well, she can't take time off during the day,' explained Dina. 'She's really keen on this place. She doesn't want to miss it.'

'Did she say what time she'd be back?' Matt was uneasy. He didn't know why but he was definitely uneasy.

'Not exactly,' said Dina. 'I can't understand why she wants to move out of here. We all get on so well together.'

'I think she just wants a bit more space,' said Matt, tactfully. 'I'll give her a ring later. Just let her know I've been round, will you?'

Matt didn't finish his coffee. It was awful. For some reason, as he drove back towards Didsbury, it was not Laura he was thinking about, it was Lydia and, as he thought of her, he could picture her face, her soft lips and her warm eyes. He hadn't heard from her for over four years. At first there had been phone calls but they were cold and formal and they soon became less frequent, eventually stopping altogether. Hardly a day had passed when he hadn't thought of her – until he met Laura, that is. Circumstance had brought Laura into his life and she had pushed Lydia out of his mind. He couldn't understand why he was thinking of Lydia now, as he drove through the rain towards Didsbury.

Matt needed petrol. He had meant to stop at the motorway services but in his haste to get home he had driven straight past. He pulled into an Esso Service Station opposite the Italian Bar in the village. He fumbled in his back pocket to see how much money he had. Ten pounds – that would have to do for now. Matt unlocked his petrol cap, slipped the nozzle in and squeezed the trigger. He watched the digital display on the pump begin to tick over, and then he looked beyond the pump, across the road to the Italian Bar with its smooth music and bright lights.

He saw them immediately. They were sitting at the same window table that he had shared with Laura on their first night. He saw them – but the fact that they were together didn't register at first. Laura was laughing and she flicked her hair back in that familiar way and shook her head, and it was only when she leaned across the table and placed her hand on Lewis' arm that Matt understood. Why Lewis of all people? He didn't know what to do. He watched as Lewis drained the last of the wine into Laura's glass and then held the bottle up as a signal for the waiter to bring another. Lewis was there with Laura, his beautiful Laura – and he didn't know what to do.

The petrol pump clicked, warning him that his tank was full. Matt stared at the display, which registered £38.50. He reached into his back pocket and took out the ten-pound note, and he stared at it forlornly.

He didn't know what to do.

Chapter 14

It was 2.00 a.m. in the morning. Matt sat alone in the living room of Number 32 Ashton Avenue with a half empty bottle of Bell's Whisky by his side. He had been given the whisky years ago and had never touched it. These days whisky depressed him.

Matt had rung Laura just before midnight. He had watched Lydia walk out of his life and he had made no effort to change her mind. He should have pleaded with her to stay. He should have followed her to London, given up his paltry little house in Didsbury and gone after her – but he did neither. He had been pathetic. He had allowed her to walk out of his life. He had no intention of making the same mistake with Laura and so he rang her, just before midnight.

Dina answered the phone. 'I'm sorry, she's not here, Matt.' And when he hadn't said anything for a few moments, she added, 'Matt, are you all right, Matt?'

Without replying, he placed the handset back on the receiver. He wasn't all right. He was desperate. It was midnight and she wasn't home and he had seen her with Lewis Jordan. Lewis Jordan of all people. How could she?

Matt poured another whisky and took a gulp. He winced and shook his head as the whisky pulled at the back of his throat. He stood up, shakily, still holding his glass, and he grabbed the bottle with his free hand. He headed for the stairs, stumbling into the coffee table on his way out of the room.

'I'm not going to let her go. No way – not to that bastard!'

At least he could still talk to himself.

The following morning, Matt rang in to A1 Computers and told them he was ill. In truth, he did feel awful. He had hardly slept. Each time he had closed his eyes he had seen images of Laura and Lewis Jordan together, staring wide-eyed at each other across the table in the Italian Bar. How could she? Why with him? Matt had finally drifted off into an uneasy, alcohol fuelled sleep in the early hours, only to wake up soon after when he rolled over onto the empty whisky bottle. His head ached and his mouth was dry. When he had first tried to stand up he had felt dizzy and he had sat back down on the bed for a few minutes to recover. Eventually, he staggered to the bathroom and when he looked in the mirror he was disgusted at what he saw. He imagined Lewis Jordan staring out of the glass at him; immaculately groomed; white teeth; clean shaven with his slick, gelled black hair and sickly smile. Matt hated him. He had never liked him but now he hated him.

Matt forced himself to eat a piece of toast and he helped it down with a mug of strong, sweet black coffee. He couldn't have put any milk in even if he'd wanted to. He had left it out on the kitchen table and it had gone off. He drew back the living room curtains and winced at the sudden infusion of light. At least it wasn't raining; it was a clear, bright morning.

Matt knew what he had to do. He just needed to talk to her. He would tell her what Lewis was like and he would make her listen, whether she wanted to or not.

He drove the short distance to Didsbury Village and paid the garage what he owed from the night before. The attendant had been pretty understanding. He knew Matt from previous visits and, besides, he had his car registration number.

Matt parked up in Sandhurst Road, next to the college, and walked the short distance to Didsbury Park. He was feeling more human by now, tired and thoroughly depressed rather than ill. The fresh air would do him good. He had bought a bottle of water from the garage and he carried it with him as he walked slowly round the gravel path that bordered the park, sipping from the plastic bottle every so often in an effort to rehydrate himself.

He had made up his mind to ring her at lunchtime and he began to rehearse aloud what he would say to her. After a few circuits of the path, he sat down on a wooden park bench that was scarred with years of graffiti. It was mid-morning and the small park was almost deserted. A group of students cut through on their way to lectures, one of them chatting away in a particularly loud voice on the obligatory mobile phone; an elderly man walked his dog, stopping to scoop up the deposit it left with a yellow, plastic spade. Matt hated the very thought of it. He couldn't imagine anything worse than scooping up fresh dog shit and carrying it around in a little plastic bag. A young mother walked past him shoving a pushchair, a whinging child struggling to escape from its straps. She hurried on when she heard Matt talking to himself.

Matt looked at his watch and was amazed to note that an hour had passed. The only line he'd settled on was: 'Hello, Laura – it's me.' After another fifteen fruitless minutes he decided that it would be better if the conversation was spontaneous and he raised himself from the bench and made his way back to the car. He sat there for a few minutes, gripping the steering wheel and staring straight ahead through the window.

He rang at five past twelve. His heart was

thumping and his mouth was dry again. The tone sounded for about thirty seconds and then cut off completely. Matt couldn't believe it. She must have looked at the display and then switched her phone off. What was the matter with her?

He decided to ring the school. He knew she didn't like personal calls at work but it was the only way to get through to her. He punched in the number and then sat back in his car seat and waited. The nervousness had gone; he was angry and frustrated.

'Good afternoon, St Gregory's Primary School.'

Matt recognised the secretary's voice and he shuffled forward in his car seat. It was important to remain calm.

'Good afternoon. Could I speak to Miss Williams, please?'

'I'll see if she's available. Who shall I say is calling?'

Matt hesitated. He thought for a moment before replying, 'Can you tell her it's the estate agent.'

'Just hold the line. I'll try to transfer you.'

He felt strangely pleased with himself. He was sure she would come to the phone. Within moments she was there and Matt froze as soon as he heard her voice.

'Hello, Laura Williams speaking.'

'Laura – it's me.'

There was a moment's pause and then she said, 'You shouldn't have rung me here, Matt. You know they don't like personal calls.'

'I had to speak to you, Laura. What's going on? I came round last night.'

'I know. Dina told me.'

'And I rang at midnight, Laura. You weren't there.'

'I'm sorry, Matt. I've got a lot on my mind at the moment. I'm trying to sort out the flat.'

'Is that what you were doing at midnight? Trying to sort out the flat?'

'I don't have to explain anything to you, Matt – not if I don't want to.' She realised she had been hard on him and she said, 'Look, things have been difficult here at work lately and – well, we just seemed to be moving too quickly.'

Matt took a deep breath. 'We don't have to move too quickly, Laura. We can move as slowly as you like as long as we just keep moving.'

'Matt, I don't know if I'm ready for any sort of long-term relationship. I never meant it to be like that. I'm moving house. I'm going to live on my own. I just want some time to myself. I don't want to hurt you, Matt.'

'And you think you're not hurting me by refusing to answer my phone calls? I was called away because my father collapsed and was rushed into hospital and you won't even answer my phone calls. He could be dead for all you know.'

'I know he's not dead, Matt. I spoke to Dina. And I'm sorry – I'm just so confused.'

'Can we meet and talk about it, Laura? Tonight, after you finish work?'

'Not tonight, Matt. I can't meet you tonight.'

'Why not? What else are you doing tonight?'

'You're doing it again, Matt. You're crowding me. I said not tonight. That should be enough.'

'It's not enough, Laura. I need to talk to you.' Matt's voice was beginning to crack. He took another deep breath. 'Everything was fine before I went to Whitby. What's happened to change things so quickly?'

'Look, Matt – I have to go. I'm due back in class. I'll get back to you, all right?'

'When, Laura? When will you get back to me? I have to talk to you.'

'I'm sorry, Matt. I have to go.'

And she put the phone down, leaving him holding his mobile to his ear, with the dialling tone droning steadily.

Chapter 15

Matt waited until nine o'clock that evening before phoning Laura at the house in Chorlton. He wasn't surprised when no one answered and he got the same result when he tried Laura's mobile. He felt sick at the thought of her with Lewis Jordan. Each time he closed his eyes he could see them together in the Italian Bar, she reaching out her hand to touch his arm, he with his smarmy black hair and false smile. He imagined Lewis driving her home in his flashy black car, the two of them going in together, his arm draped around her shoulders, and him waking up besides her the next morning. He could almost hear her saying, *'You won't like me in the morning,'* and he knew that Lewis would love to wake up to her in the morning, just as he had done. He couldn't stand the thought of it. That had been the best thing for Matt, waking up beside her the following morning.

Matt couldn't sit still. He wandered into the kitchen and opened the fridge, but the very thought of food made him feel sick. It was just as well that the fridge was almost empty. He closed the door and sauntered over to the window. He was desperate to see her. He missed Laura and he wanted her with him.

Matt couldn't stay in on his own. He thought about going for a walk in the cold night air. Maybe he could go back to Didsbury Park and sit on that same bench where he had tried to plan his phone call to Laura. It hadn't worked last time, it probably wouldn't work again. Besides, he was beginning to get a complex about people staring at him as if he was some kind of weirdo.

He rejected that idea and, out of desperation, he decided to ring Beano instead. The tone sounded for a few seconds and then Beano's answering machine cut in.

Matt waited in frustration as the recorded message rambled on and then he said, 'Beano, it's me, Matt. I was hoping we could go for a drink. I need to talk to you.' He thought for a minute and then he added, 'If you're coming, I'll be at The Old Cock. Come and join me, will you?'

Matt put the phone down and cursed his luck. 'The one time I need him,' he said out loud, 'and he's not fucking there!' He pulled on a jacket and went out into the ever-present November drizzle.

Matt arrived at The Old Cock within fifteen minutes. He glanced around the tables and, although there were some familiar faces, there was no one he knew well enough to sit with. He felt awkward. He and Beano used to laugh when they saw characters in pubs who were obviously on their own, sad bastards who stood at the bar and tried to engage in conversation with anyone who was stupid enough to go near them.

Matt walked across and stood at the bar, shuffling his feet uneasily. He felt sure that he was being watched but when he glanced around nobody seemed to be interested in him. He almost felt disappointed. That was the story of his life – nobody seemed to be interested in him. Even Beano, with his stained trousers and sad hair, had let him down when he most needed a friend.

Matt turned back to the bar to see the new barmaid standing in front of him. She didn't say anything – she just stood there chewing gum.

'Pint of bitter, please,' said Matt, and he put two pounds and a fifty pence coin down on the bar.

'It's gone up,' she said, staring at the coins. 'I need another twelve pence.'

Matt fished in his pocket and placed another fifty pence piece on the bar.

The girl pulled his pint, delivered his change and disappeared out of view. She hadn't spoken another word. Matt sipped his bitter and thought about Laura. The problem was, the more he thought about the situation, the more he could understand Laura falling for Lewis Jordan. Lewis was everything that Matt was not. He was confident and good-looking; he wore smart designer clothes and he drove a fast car; he was clearly successful in his job and destined for great things. There was no way Laura was going to look at them both and choose Matt. Why choose milk when you can have cream? Lewis Jordan could probably pull any girl he wanted and yet the bastard had gone for Laura. But there was no way Matt was going to give her up. He had made that mistake with Lydia. For once in his life he was going to fight for something that he really wanted.

Matt glanced at his glass and saw that it was nearly empty. He drained the last drops and signalled to the barmaid for a refill. As she was filling his pint, he looked beyond her to the row of optics, neatly lined in front of a large mirror. There were several whiskies, both blends and malts. At the very end of the row was a bottle of Southern Comfort. No, he shook his head remembering again that whisky made him feel depressed. He felt bad enough already. Southern Comfort! Matt hadn't tasted Southern Comfort for years – probably not since his time at university. These days the youngsters drank Jack Daniels if they wanted to dabble in whisky. As he stared at the distinctive bottle, Matt remembered a party thrown by a group of the girls at uni. They shared a flat together somewhere in Didsbury –

he couldn't recall exactly where. The night had begun at The Old Cock and they had taken over a whole section of the pub. Beano was there and by eleven o'clock, tired of the bulk of bitter, the two of them were drinking Southern Comfort. Matt vaguely remembered pairing off with a girl who had cropped black hair and wore bright red lipstick – but that's all he remembered. That was just typical of sad Matthew Hudson – the one time he had copped off he couldn't even remember it! Somehow, Beano had got him back to the hall of residence and forced him to drink a pint of water. He could hear Beano's voice now: 'You'll be all right in the morning if you down a pint of water before you sleep.' Matt wasn't all right. He was violently sick in the night and he felt like a dog the next day. He hadn't touched Southern Comfort since. That was the trouble with Beano – you couldn't believe a word he said.

Matt suddenly realised that the barmaid was waiting for her money. He pulled a ten pound note from his pocket and said, 'And I'll have a Southern Comfort as well, please. In fact, make it a double.'

Over an hour had passed and there was still no sign of Beano. Matt had downed another pint and chased it with a double Southern Comfort. His head was beginning to feel strangely numb and the background noise of the pub seemed to be some distance away. Nobody had spoken to him. He was twenty-nine years old, he drank on his own in pubs and mothers with young children avoided him in parks.

Matt was aware of somebody brushing against him and he glanced round to see the student, the same student he and Beano had watched down a pint of lager in front of his friends a week ago, walking towards the gents toilet. Matt watched as the student pushed the door open, and he noticed that a couple of other youths followed in behind.

Matt suddenly realised that he needed the toilet himself. He had downed three pints and several Southern Comforts and he hadn't been to the toilet once. He drained the last drop of whisky from his glass, steadied himself, and headed towards the toilet door. He reached out a hand to push the door inwards but before he made contact it flew open and a rush of bodies barged past him, knocking him sideways. There were two or three . . . Matt wasn't sure – but he recognised the last one through the door. Their eyes met for a few fleeting seconds and there was instant recognition. It was the Afro-Caribbean kid; the one Matt had helped when he was attacked at Chorlton Bus Station. And then he was gone, after the others, through the bar and out of the pub.

Matt shook his head and carried on into the toilets. He heard the groans immediately and he knew there was a problem. The student was on the stone floor, slumped against one of the cubicle doors. He was in a mess. His face was smeared with blood and his right eye was swelling even as Matt stared at him. Matt couldn't move for a moment. He just stood and stared at the student as if he were an injured animal.

The toilet door opened again and one of the student's friends walked in. He went to push past Matt and then stopped in horror.

'Shit! What's going on?' He edged forward towards his friend and then turned and looked with suspicion towards Matt.

'It wasn't me,' said Matt, defensively. 'He's been mugged. Black kids. They've just run out.'

It wasn't real. It was as if he was watching the scene on a TV screen.

'Well, don't just stand there, man! Get some help!'

Matt came to his senses and hurried back to the bar. He pushed in between a group of people ordering drinks and shouted for the new girl to fetch the landlord, and then he went back to check on the student. He was just coming round, his friend crouched by his side. He had pulled himself up into a sitting position, his back resting on the toilet door. His friend had dampened a paper towel and had wiped the blood away from his mouth. It was smeared across his cheek and his chin. The swelling near his eye was the size of an egg.

The landlord entered, a big man with a

shock of brown hair and a moustache. He knelt down by the lad.

'Are you all right, son? I've sent for the police.'

'I'm all right,' confirmed the student, and a dribble of blood and saliva trickled from his mouth when he spoke. 'Bastards! Bloody bastards! They've stolen my mobile phone!'

Chapter 16

Matt had overslept. It hadn't been a restful sleep. He had woken up at about two in the morning desperately in need of the toilet. He had stumbled to the bathroom feeling pretty dreadful, suddenly remembering why he hadn't bothered with Southern Comfort for so many years. He had fallen back into bed, covered in a cold sweat that made him shake and groan out loud in discomfort. And then the dreams had arrived; grotesque, disturbed dreams that seemed to swim around his head in confusion. He saw his father, old and gaunt, lying in a hospital bed, his mother bent forward over the covers, crying steadily. He saw Dina lying naked, handcuffed to the metal bed post, writhing and screaming for help as he himself stood in the corner of the room holding a huge metal key. He saw the student lying bloodied on the toilet floor and, as he stared at him, his face changed into Lewis' smarmy, grinning face, and Matt kicked him and laughed uncontrollably. But he didn't see Laura. He was searching for her amidst the confusion and she was nowhere to be found. He was shouting out her name over and over again in despair, his voice echoing and trailing away into the distance. He was walking into a thick, swirling grey mist with his arms outstretched and when he came out of the mist, he woke with a start. He had overslept.

Matt put two pieces of bread into the toaster as he got ready for work. He felt terrible but he was getting used to the feeling. He could cope. He hadn't time for a shave. He buttered the toast and took a few gulps of milk straight from the plastic bottle and then he left for work. He would eat the toast as he drove.

Matt knew what he had to do. He had to see Laura. He had to speak to her face to face and make her understand how good they would be together. She wasn't answering his phone calls and he knew that she would be with Lewis in the evening, so he would go to the school and he would talk to her there. He had made up his mind. He was going to go to St Gregory's School that very lunchtime. Satisfied with his plan, he took a bite of cold toast. It tasted awful, like dry cardboard. He couldn't chew it. Matt pressed the button to lower his window and he threw his toast out into the street.

The morning went slowly. He called in at base, which was on the second floor of a modern office block a couple of miles outside Didsbury, towards the city centre, and picked up his job card. He only had a couple of calls to make that morning. Good. He could time it so that he got to the school for about twelve-thirty. That way he could catch Laura on her lunch break.

The first job was easy. Matt had installed a system for a firm of solicitors in Gately and he was booked in to perform a health check. The only problem seemed to be that the senior partner of Norris and Blunt had an inbred hatred of computers and refused to touch the new fangled machines that had invaded the privacy of his chambers.

'Can't see the point of them!' snapped Crispin Norris, from behind a pair of brown-rimmed spectacles. 'Anything I want to know I can find in a book, thank you very much. And books aren't half as temperamental as these bloody machines!'

Where had Crispin Norris been for the last twenty years? Matt smiled politely and got on with his check. It took him about forty-five minutes and then he moved on to his next job – a problem with the networking system in a telesales department for fitted doors and windows. Standing outside the front entrance, Matt realised that it was the very same fitted doors and windows company that Beano had graced for the first three full weeks of his working life. The firm couldn't be too bad – it had had the sense to sack Beano. Matt hated those junk calls that always seemed to come as he was sitting down to eat after work. He particularly hated calls from firms selling windows.

'Hello, Mr Hudson? Don't worry – I'm not trying to sell you anything – but what would you say if I told you that you could have any two windows replaced absolutely free? You see, we're promoting our company in the area and we're looking for . . .'

Matt never let them get any further. It was the one area in which he was decisive – probably because he didn't have to deal with the caller face-to-face. The irony was that Matt needed all his windows replaced. He just couldn't be bothered to get the job organised.

The networking problem proved difficult and Matt was in no mood to spend too much time with a double glazing firm. Matt explained to the supervisor that he would have to return with some replacement components and promised that the system would be up and running within twenty-four hours. He had no intention of keeping that promise.

By twelve o'clock Matt was back in Didsbury. He was feeling better and his stomach was rumbling. That was a good sign. He picked up a cheese and pickle sandwich and a bottle of water from a small bakery in the village and drove the short distance to St Gregory's School.

Matt didn't enter the car park. He stopped in the road outside, opposite the school playground. All of a sudden, as he watched the children chasing around the yard, laughing and shouting and screaming, his confidence seemed to disappear. Perhaps it wasn't such a good idea after all, turning up at school. Laura didn't even like him phoning. She would be horrified to see him there in person.

And then she was there, in front of him, in the schoolyard. She was wearing tracksuit bottoms and a loose maroon sweatshirt embroidered with the school emblem, and she had a group of the older girls gathered around her, changed into short skirts and tops, ready for netball practice. Matt felt his heartbeat quicken. He watched as Laura organised the girls into two teams and set the game in motion.

She was in complete control, directing and coaching and encouraging, stopping them every so often to emphasize a teaching point. She brought girls on and off the court, swapped them round and demonstrated moves herself, every so often. She was in complete control and, as Matt watched her, he began to wonder if they really were suited, for he couldn't think of a single part of his life that he controlled to his satisfaction. But that was why he was there, outside the school – to take control of his life.

After about fifteen minutes, Laura blew her whistle and gathered the girls around her. They squatted down to rest and to talk about the game. Matt couldn't see them properly so he got out of his car and wandered across to the wire mesh fence that surrounded the playground. He would catch her attention when the practice was finished.

Laura didn't notice him. She blew her whistle and the game restarted. After a few minutes Matt was aware of a small figure standing directly in front of him, inside the playground. He glanced down to see George, hands on hips, staring up at him, a puzzled expression on his freckled face. His friend was a few paces behind, hands in pockets.

'Hello, Mister. Have you come about the computer again?'

'Hello, George.' Matt remembered his name. How could he forget? 'No, I was hoping to have a word with your teacher, Miss Williams.'

'She's busy,' said George, without looking round. 'She's doing a netball practice.'

'I can see that,' replied Matt, taking a deep breath, 'but I really need to speak to her.'

'Do you want me to get her for you? We'll be going back to class in a few minutes.'

Before Matt could answer, a large lady wearing a blue overall approached and took hold of the boy's hand. Matt guessed that she was one of the lunchtime supervisors.

'Come on, George. What are you doing over here?' She glanced towards Matt as she edged George away from the fence.

'I'm talking to the computer man,' protested

George. 'He wants to speak to Miss Williams.'

'Well, you go and play over there,' insisted the supervisor, shoving him towards the school building, 'and I'll deal with it, should I?' And turning back to Matt, she said, 'Can I help, at all?'

She was looking at him most suspiciously. He was dishevelled and unshaven and she had spotted him staring across at the girls playing netball.

Matt was embarrassed. He hadn't meant to draw attention to himself.

'Er . . . no, thanks. I just need a word with Laura – Miss Williams. I was waiting until she'd finished the practice.'

Laura had seen him. She had blown the whistle and she had stopped the game and she was walking across the yard towards him.

'It's OK, Jean, I'll deal with this,' she said, putting a reassuring hand on the supervisor's arm.

Jean turned away and walked back into the yard looking most uncomfortable.

Laura was annoyed. 'What are you doing here, Matt? Why are you here?'

'You won't answer my calls. I've got to talk to you, Laura.'

'I'm in the middle of a netball practice, Matt. I'm with the children.' She glanced around and indicated with her arm.

The netball girls were grouped together in the middle of the yard. They were staring across and one or two of them were giggling.

'I can't talk now, Matt. I'm at work. You shouldn't have come.'

'Well, when, Laura? Tell me when we can talk?'

He was becoming agitated. This was not what he had planned.

'I don't know, Matt. I'll call you. We'll sort something out.'

Laura began to move away but Matt was not going to let it drop. 'You said that last time, Laura. You said you'd call me and you didn't.' His voice was rising. He could feel a lump in his throat and his heart was pounding. 'I'm still waiting, Laura. I'm still waiting for your call.'

Matt was shouting. He had moved forward and his hands were gripping the wire mesh fence. The whole playground had gone silent. Everyone was looking in his direction.

Laura continued to walk away. 'How could you do this to me, Matt? Go away! Leave me alone!'

The lunchtime supervisor made a decision. She blew her whistle and shouted for the children to move inside. One of the other teachers appeared in the yard to help usher in the children.

'Laura! Laura!' He was shaking the fence as he watched her start to run across the yard in tears.

A small voice broke his concentration. It was George. He had wandered back across towards the fence to offer some advice.

'It's all right, Mister. You needn't worry. The computer's been fine since you fixed it.'

The lunchtime supervisor rushed across and whisked him away, glaring at Matt, who was stretched against the wire mesh fence, distraught.

The playground was deserted. A few empty crisp packets and some crinkled autumn leaves blew across the tarmac. Two large, black crows circled overhead and then swooped down to scavenge some crumbs that had spilled from one of the crisp packets. Matt still stood with his hands on the fence, staring across the yard. He could see faces in the staffroom window. Someone had pulled the vertical blind to one side and there were several faces staring across at him as if he were an escaped animal. He recognised the secretary. She was holding a cup of tea in one hand and she was pointing at him with the other. There was no sign of Laura.

After a few minutes, a police car drew up, silently, and parked behind Matt's car. Two officers got out and began to walk across towards him. He heard one of their radios, muffled and harsh, like a railway station announcement. Still he stared into the empty yard. He didn't move.

One of the officers put a hand on his shoulder.

'What's all this about, mate? You shouldn't be here, should you?'

Matt turned his head and looked at him. He didn't say a word.

'A domestic, is it? Have you had a bit of a problem with the Missus or the girlfriend?'

'Something like that,' said Matt, quietly. He let go of the fence at last. He suddenly felt cold and he began to shiver. 'I'm sorry. I didn't mean to cause a problem. I just wanted to talk to her. It all went wrong.'

'I tell you what,' said the officer, taking hold of his arm and leading him firmly away from the fence, 'let's go across to the car and we'll have a chat about it, should we?'

Matt made no attempt to resist. He was completely compliant. His energy was spent.

Chapter 17

The two police officers handled the situation well. Matt had regained control quickly and he made a full apology for his performance. It wasn't like him; he had never been in trouble with the police. He had been worried when they had insisted on breathalysing him, especially when they realised that Matt had driven to the school. Matt half expected the result to be positive from the amount he had drunk the night before but, to his relief, it was clear. They took all his details and left him in no doubt whatsoever what would happen to him if he turned up at the school again. They waited as he got into his car and drove away, and Matt was aware that they followed him for a short distance before shooting off in a different direction.

As soon as the police car was out of sight, Matt pulled into a side road and stopped. He unfastened his seat belt, leaned forward onto the steering wheel and put his head in his hands.

'What have I done! What have I done!' He hit the steering wheel in frustration. 'Bloody stupid sod! What have I done!'

He sat in the car for half an hour, going over and over the scene at the school in his mind. Hindsight was wonderful. He knew just how he should have handled it; what he should have said and how he should have reacted. But it hadn't happened. He blew it and he wouldn't blame Laura if she never spoke to him again.

He caught sight of himself in the rear view mirror, his eyes red and tired, his face unshaven, his hair dishevelled and badly in need of a wash, and he thought of the immaculate Lewis Jordan and cursed out loud.

Matt knew he should ring in to the office to see if any more jobs had come in but, instead, he made a decision. He would go and see Beano. He desperately needed a friend and Beano was still off work with a bad back. He could talk to Beano and confide in him and even ask his advice. He didn't have to take it – but he could ask.

Matt drove the short distance back to Didsbury and pulled up outside Beano's flat. It wasn't wonderful; three rooms above a greengrocer's shop in a side road on the Manchester side of the village. At least he got plenty of fresh fruit and vegetables – much better than the weetabix curry he used to live off in his early working life. The result was similar, though. Matt was constantly hearing about the effect all the fresh fruit had on Beano. It was even worse when it was accompanied by a heavy night of bitter drinking.

It was a corner shop and the entrance to Beano's flat was around the side, a green door that complemented the produce on sale. Matt locked the car and rang the push button bell at the side of the green door. He waited a couple of minutes and when there was no response, he rang it again.

Matt took a few steps back from the door and stared up at the window. The vertical blind was pulled to one side and Beano's face appeared, anxious and inquisitive. Matt waved a hand and then pointed to the door as a signal to be let in. Beano waved back and nodded.

It was a few more minutes before the green door was opened. Matt didn't wait to be invited in. He pushed past his friend and headed for the stairs that led up to Beano's flat.

'Matt . . .' began Beano, following immediately, 'I . . . er . . . didn't expect to see you today. I mean, aren't you at work? You don't usually call round in the middle of the afternoon.'

'I've made a bloody fool of myself, Beano.' Matt climbed the stairs and Beano followed. 'I went round to Laura's school and made a bloody fool of myself. I can't believe I did it!' Matt walked straight through into Beano's flat and sat down in an armchair that had been covered with a multicoloured throw-over. 'Shit! I can't believe I did it!'

'Come on, Matt. It's probably not as bad

as you think.'

Beano pushed the living room door closed behind him and sat down opposite his friend. Matt noticed that Beano had treated himself to a new pair of trousers. He had no shoes or socks on but the trousers were new and his T-shirt was clean.

'Beano – the only girl I've had for years, the only girl I really care about has just dumped me, she's shagging Lewis Jordan and you're trying to tell me it's not as bad as I think! For Christ's sake!'

'I see what you mean,' said Beano, scratching his chin. 'Well, if you're right, it just shows that she's got no taste. She's not worth bothering about, is she? You've got to put her out of your mind, Matt. Move on.'

'It took me five bloody years to move on from Lydia.'

Matt stood up and walked across to the window. He put his hands in his pockets and stared down to the street.

'I can't move on, Beano. I don't want to move on. I want Laura.'

'Look, Matt – why don't we get together for a drink and talk about it, eh? Perhaps now's not the time. Give yourself a day or so to think about the situation and then we'll get together for a drink. What d'you say?'

Matt turned and looked around the room. Something wasn't right. It took him a few minutes to realise what it was. It was too tidy and there wasn't the usual peculiar smell pervading the flat. Matt glanced at Beano's new trousers and he moved forward, slowly. He prodded Beano and stared straight into his eyes.

'What are you up to, Beano? What's going on?'

Before Beano could answer, the door to the bedroom opened and a figure dressed in nothing more than a large T-shirt stepped through.

'Hello, Matt,' said Dina. 'I bet you didn't expect to see me here, eh?'

'Bloody hell!' said Matt. He was stunned. He stared straight ahead and then he repeated the words again. 'Bloody hell, Beano! I thought you had a bad back!'

Dina walked across to the armchair and sat down. The T-shirt only just protected her modesty.

'Well, at least you've got more on than last time I saw you!' said Matt. 'Bloody hell, Beano! Why didn't you say something?'

'I was going to tell you,' said Beano, 'honest I was. But the timing didn't seem right. Not with you having problems with Laura, and all that.'

'You should have told me,' repeated Matt. 'I can't take too many more shocks, Beano.'

'I'm sorry about you and Laura,' interrupted Dina. 'You're just right for her. I don't like that other guy.'

'Perhaps you should tell that to Laura,' said Matt. 'Is she serious about him?'

'I don't know,' said Dina. 'It's hard to tell. She's spending a lot of time with him but I don't think it will last. He'll let her down. His type always let you down.'

'I wouldn't let her down,' said Matt. 'How can I prove to her that I wouldn't let her down?'

'Perhaps that's what she's frightened of,' said Dina. 'I don't think she's ready to make a commitment.'

Dina sat forward and her T-shirt rode up even more. Matt averted his eyes.

'Look, Matt,' said Beano, 'I don't want to be awkward but do you think we could talk about this some other time? It's just that . . .'

'Yes, I understand,' interrupted Matt, and he moved towards the door. 'You give me a call, eh? And, er . . . have a nice afternoon.'

Despite all of his troubles, Matt couldn't help but smile as he shook his head and descended the stairs in disbelief.

Chapter 18

'What the bloody hell were you playing at outside St Gregory's School this lunchtime?'

It was Brendan Clough, Matt's boss at A1 Computers. He was steaming. Matt held the phone away from his ear as Brendan continued to rant.

'Are you some sort of weirdo or something, watching the little children in the school playground?'

'It wasn't like that, Brendan. It was personal. There was a personal problem I had to sort out.'

'You've got a bloody bigger problem now, mate. I've had an official complaint from the Headteacher. She doesn't want you anywhere near the building again, do you understand?'

'I understand,' said Matt. 'I'm sorry, Brendan.'

'And she's contacted the Local Education Authority. Bloody hell, Matt – we could lose the schools' contract because of you! Tens of thousands of pounds worth of work! If that happens, you're looking for another job. Do you understand?'

'I understand,' repeated Matt. 'I'm really sorry. I won't go near the place again.'

Matt didn't really care but he knew it was better to humour Brendan.

'And you get yourself to the office tomorrow morning,' continued Brendan. He wasn't shouting quite so much. 'Where the hell were you this afternoon? You need to sort yourself out, Matt. Get your act together.'

'I'll be at the office first thing in the morning,' said Matt, 'and I'm sorry about today.'

He put the phone down before Brendan could come back at him and he slumped back in his chair. He knew he should have gone to the office after leaving Beano's flat but he just couldn't face it. He had left the car outside the greengrocer's shop and walked. He had walked up to the Italian Bar and stared in the window, remembering how he had sat there with Laura, how easy it had been to talk to her and how they had laughed together. He couldn't understand why she wouldn't talk to him now. That was the worst thing. She had given him no explanation. He didn't know what he had done wrong. He walked through the village, past Didsbury Park and the college, and he stopped opposite The Old Cock Inn. He leaned against a wall and stared across the road to the pub and he remembered how he had chatted clumsily to Laura on the night he had asked her out, and how fantastic he had felt when she had agreed to meet him. He wondered, for a moment, whether he should cross the road and go in for a few drinks, just to calm himself down, just to help him get things in perspective. And then he remembered how he'd felt after a night on Southern Comfort and he banished any thought of a repeat performance from his mind.

He walked a bit further, towards West Didsbury and the railway station and, as he walked, he remembered what Laura was like in the morning, how soft and warm when she was lying next to him, and he couldn't bear to think of her waking up next to Lewis Jordan. It was tearing him apart, not being with her – and he knew he had to give it one more try. Even though she probably hated him for showing her up at St Gregory's, he just knew he had to try again.

Laura had been sent home early from school. She had sat in Mrs Nelson's room, her mind in turmoil, swimming with a mixture of different emotions. She felt upset because she had handled the situation badly. It was her fault. If only she had plucked up the courage to speak to Matt earlier he would never have turned up outside school. She felt embarrassed that everyone had seen the confrontation – especially the children. How could she face the children? She felt a hint of pity that she had hurt Matt and reduced him to such a state but, most of all, she felt anger, a burning, devouring anger. How dare he turn up at the school and create such a scene! He had no right to approach her in that way. What did he think he was doing?

'Things to sort out,' said Mrs Nelson in her usual abrupt manner. She was not the sympathetic sort. 'Can't have all this fuss happening again, Laura – especially in front of the children. They see quite enough of that at home!'

'I'm sorry, Mrs Nelson,' Laura had replied, her voice trembling with emotion. 'I can assure you it won't happen again. You have my word.'

'Yes, well I hope you're right. Can't let your personal problems overflow into school. It just won't work, Laura. Now get yourself off home for the afternoon. I'll make sure your class is covered.'

Laura had not argued. The thought of being interrogated by George was enough to convince her that Mrs Nelson's advice was the right course of action to take. It was when she entered the cold, empty house that emotion overcame her. It seemed more untidy than ever; the ashtray overflowing; the smell of stale cigarettes pervading the air; the clothes maiden laden with damp underwear. How had she got herself into such a mess? She sank slowly onto the sofa and buried her head in her hands. As she sobbed uncontrollably, she couldn't get the image out of her mind – Matt hanging onto the school fence, his eyes wide with hurt, calling out her name over and over again. She suddenly realised that she wanted him. She needed comfort. More than ever, she needed someone to hold her and caress her and tell her that they cared. Laura wiped the tears from her eyes. She picked up the phone and she dialled Lewis' number.

It was nine o'clock. Matt had smartened himself up. He had showered and he had shaved and, when he looked in the mirror, a reasonably human face had stared back at him. The eyes were still a bit red but that wouldn't be too noticeable in the dark. He had opened the wardrobe and pulled out his black trousers and maroon shirt – the same maroon shirt he'd worn at the Italian Bar with Laura. There was still a slight stain on it where Matt had wiped the black kid's blood off his hands – but it was hardly noticeable, especially underneath his jacket. It blended in with his shirt. Matt gave himself a final squirt from an almost empty can of Lynx, picked up his car keys and left the house.

He was feeling quite confident again. As he drove towards Laura's house in Chorlton, he felt completely in control. He rehearsed the scene in his head. If she wasn't in, he would post the letter of apology he had written through the letterbox and try again the next evening. But if she was at home, he would remain very calm. He would show her he was in control. He would apologise for embarrassing her and he would ask to be let in to her house. That was the first hurdle – getting through the door of her house. Once inside, she would offer him a coffee and they would talk. He knew if he could get her talking he was in with a chance. He would take things slowly but he wouldn't leave until he had arranged to see her again. Matt went over all this in his mind and he was convinced it would work.

He turned into Laura's road, opposite the bus station – and his plan was blown apart. There was Lewis Jordan's black Audi parked outside the house. He was inside with Laura and Matt didn't know what to do. He pulled over to the opposite side of the road and switched off the car engine. His confidence had evaporated and he was shaking like a leaf.

Matt looked across to the house and noticed that there was only one light on, downstairs in the front room. He guessed that both Meg and Dina were out. Meg was likely to be on duty at the hospital and Dina was probably doing something horrible with Beano. That meant that Laura and Lewis were alone together in the front room. He knew what he should do. He should post the letter and drive straight home – but Matt had no intention of taking that course of action.

He sat there for ten minutes, watching the window, gradually growing more and more agitated, and then he got out of the car and walked across the road to Laura's front door. He stood on the step and took a deep breath. His heart was pounding and he could feel the sweat forming on his brow. Matt knew he was doing the wrong thing even before he rang the bell but he couldn't stop himself. She was in there, with Lewis and he had to see her. Matt had lost his composure. It had disappeared the moment he had spotted Lewis' car. He could feel himself getting more and more irritated as he left his finger on the push button bell.

And then the hall light went on and a figure moved towards the front door. Matt knew that it was Laura and he suddenly realised in a panic that he had forgotten all the words he had rehearsed so thoroughly.

The door opened and she was there, in front of him, dressed in denims and a short-sleeved jumper that tantalisingly revealed a section of her midriff.

Before he could utter a word Laura took a step backwards and said, 'Matt, what are you doing to me? I don't believe you're here!'

'I'm sorry, Laura, I had to see you. I – I told you, we need to talk.' He was aware that his voice trembled. His confidence had evaporated. 'That's the least you owe me.'

'I don't owe you anything, Matt. And I told you that I'd call you,' said Laura. 'I can't believe what you did today, Matt. I couldn't go back in to class. How could you turn up and humiliate me?'

'I'm so sorry, Laura. I didn't mean it to be like that. I just need to know what's gone wrong between us.'

'Nothing's gone wrong, Matt. I wasn't aware I'd made a lifetime commitment. It was just fun, Matt. I would have been in touch – but you're so intense. I don't want that, Matt. Now, please – will you go away. It's not convenient, Matt.'

Before he could reply, Lewis appeared at Laura's shoulder. He was looking immaculate as usual; a brushed denim shirt, the top three buttons unfastened to display a plain gold chain, a smug look on his face.

'Are you all right, Laura? Is there a problem?'

'No, it's OK, Lewis. This is Matt. I told you about Matt.'

Lewis' expression changed immediately. He edged in front of Laura.

'You've got some nerve. What are you doing here?'

'That's my business. I've come to talk to Laura, not you.'

Lewis bristled. 'Go inside, Laura. I'll deal with this.'

'It's all right, Lewis. I can handle things.'

'I said go inside, Laura.'

'Why don't you let her make up her own

mind,' said Matt, and he suddenly felt more confident again.

Lewis' fist came from nowhere. It smacked into Matt's face and sent him reeling backwards. He staggered for a few brief seconds and then crumpled to the floor. He could taste the blood straight away. It was in his mouth and in his throat and, as he knelt forward on all fours, it began to drip steadily onto the wet path.

Laura screamed.

'No, Lewis! No!'

Matt's head was spinning. He couldn't focus on anything. He felt dizzy and sick and he thought he was going to black out altogether. He heard the door slam shut and he was left there, crouching on the path in the steady drizzle.

It was the cold drizzle that brought him round. Matt twisted into a sitting position and reached into his pocket for a handkerchief. He dabbed it gingerly against his nose. The whole side of his face throbbed but the bleeding had already stopped. He just sat there, cross-legged on the wet path, and the first thing he thought of was his shirt.

'That's ruined it this time,' he muttered, and he actually smiled to himself until he realised that it hurt.

Chapter 19

Matt had had a sleepless night. It was not so much that he had been thinking of Laura, it was more that his face throbbed and ached and he had to lie in bed on his back. He never slept on his back, it made him snore. He had tried an ice pack on the swelling – well, a packet of frozen garden peas – but nobody had told him how much it hurt. It wasn't like that in the films. Five minutes with an ice pack and the swelling disappeared. Matt checked in the bathroom mirror at about six in the morning. There was a large, dark maroon area to the left of his nose but it was no worse than when he had gone to bed, so he decided to go into work. He couldn't bear the thought of staying in the house on his own. Work was the best option.

'What the fuck's happened to you?' Brendan Clough wasn't the most tactful of people. 'You look awful. Been involved in a playground scrap, have you? That's what happens when you hang around school yards.'

Matt hadn't bothered to reply. He collected his job card and returned to the car. At least he still had a job. He scanned down the list of calls and even managed a smile as he noticed the fitted kitchen shop in Chorlton was third on the list. It was good to know that some things in life never changed.

Matt parked up in Salisbury Road that lunchtime, as he had done the previous morning before his disastrous visit to Laura's school. He watched as the students spilled out of the college gates and headed off down into the village. It seemed so long ago that he was a student. It was a world away. And yet when he was there, at university, those three years seemed to stretch on forever.

Matt had considered calling in on Beano, just to bring him up to date with events, but his last visit there hadn't exactly been a great success either. Beano probably had better things to do at the moment. No, he would walk in the park on his own and gather his thoughts together.

It was cold and damp but at least the drizzle had let up for a while. Was it really just twenty-four hours ago that he had paced the same gravel path, carefully planning what he would say to win Laura back? This time it was different. Something had changed inside him and he felt calm and more in control. Maybe Lewis Jordan had done him a favour. Maybe he had just needed a good thumping to bring him to his senses. He had survived for twenty-nine years without Laura.

He would put her out of his mind and get on with his life – his boring, mediocre life.

For some reason, Matt's thoughts drifted back to Whitby and to his school days. There had been a maths teacher, Mr Mason, who always wore a brown jacket with leather patches on the elbows. There was always one teacher that the kids tormented and at Whitby Grammar School it was Mr Mason. Matt had been carried along with the other children – after all, it was only a bit of fun. What harm could it do? And so, they had stuck labels on his back, burped and farted in his lessons, flicked ink at him and even locked him in a stockroom cupboard. What was it that made Matt think of Mr Mason as he walked slowly around Didsbury Park? Was it the fact that all the children knew he lived in a pokey terraced house on the outskirts of town all on his own, without a wife to look after him? Or maybe it was because Matt finally appreciated that Mr Mason was one of life's victims and as such he could identify with him. It was only now, all these years later, that Matt felt sorry for Mr Mason.

Matt walked five times around the gravel path that bordered the park and then he returned to his car. He took a swig from the bottle of water that he always kept at his side in the pocket of the door and he turned on the engine. He would go back to Whitby at the weekend. He would ring that evening and make the arrangements. He would stay in the small attic room at Henrietta Street, where he had slept as a child, and he would look out of the window, across the rooftops to the harbour and the sea. It wasn't really running away. It would give him time and space to gather his thoughts. Besides, there was that young nurse at the hospital . . .

Matt had not eaten. He had tried – but the side of his face throbbed too much when he moved his jaw so he settled on a cup-a-soup. It was quite revolting, a deep, unnatural red colour that was supposed to represent tomatoes but not surprisingly reminded him of clotted blood. Still, at least it slid down easily. It was ten o'clock and Matt always watched the news at ten o'clock, if he wasn't out drinking with Beano. He flicked the remote control and settled down in readiness to be even more depressed. The dramatic title music sounded, the newscaster snapped out the main headlines – and Matt's front door bell rang.

He knew it would be Beano, probably coming to apologise for the other afternoon. He'd give some long, rambling explanation and then sit down and drink Matt's beer. Matt really couldn't be bothered. He let the bell sound again before he got up reluctantly and made his way to the front door. It jammed again as he tried to pull it open. It had been so damp it was sticking worse than ever.

He really would have to sort that out. Matt tugged at the handle and the door jerked open, making him stumble backwards. And when he looked, there was Laura, a few paces back, standing on the path in the semi-darkness.

She didn't say anything for a moment, and Matt was unable to speak. And then she stepped forward and said, 'Hello, Matt. I'm sorry about what happened to you. I've come to see if you're all right.'

Matt didn't answer. He just held onto the door and stared at her.

'I'm all right,' he said, eventually. 'Thanks for coming.'

She waited a moment and when nothing happened, she said, 'Can I come inside? You said you wanted to talk.'

'Yes – I'm sorry. Come on in.' And he held the door to one side as Laura, head down, walked past him into the hallway.

The newscaster was still speaking in the background. Matt had turned the sound down but he had left the TV on.

'I didn't know whether to come or not,' began Laura. 'I didn't know if you'd want to see me after last night. I'm so sorry, Matt.'

'Of course I want to see you,' said Matt. He had resigned himself to never seeing her again.

'I probably asked for it. I should have known better.'

'He shouldn't have hit you, Matt. I didn't mean for Lewis to hit you.'

'Forget it. I'll survive. Anyway, I shouldn't have come round in the first place. I should have got the message. It was just the way it all happened, Laura. I've been dumped before. In fact, I'm getting used to it. But it was just the way it happened. Why couldn't you tell me?'

Laura looked down at the floor. She fiddled with the tassel on her fleece and then she flicked her hair back and Matt felt a lump in his throat.

'Everything was so good the last time I saw you. We were getting on so well together, Laura. How could things change so quickly?'

'I'm just so mixed up at the moment.' She let go of the tassel and rubbed her forehead anxiously. Matt noticed the tears welling in her eyes. 'It wasn't you, Matt – it was work and the house and – well, it was me. When we first went out together you seemed so easy and relaxed and – undemanding. It was just what I needed at the time and it was working really well. And then before I knew what was happening I was staying over at your place and there just seemed too much expectation. I could see myself falling into another routine, another situation I wasn't sure I really wanted. And then when you were called away I met Lewis. I suppose I saw him as an escape route at first – but now it's something more. I'm not very good at dealing with people, Matt. That's a bit worrying, being a teacher, isn't it?'

'How did you meet him? Lewis Jordan, I mean.'

'He's an estate agent. I went to look around a flat and Lewis was there. He's not like anyone I've ever met before, Matt. He's different.'

'You can say that again,' said Matt, and Laura frowned at him and fiddled with her tassel again.

'Anyway, he thinks he knows you from somewhere. He recognised you when he hit you.'

'Oh, that's great,' said Matt, sarcastically. 'I'm glad he didn't flatten a complete stranger!' And then he added, 'I knew him from University. We were in the same year together. He was a prat then.'

'What are you going to do?' said Laura, anxiously. 'You need to keep out of his way. He's got a temper. I don't want you to get hurt, Matt.'

'Don't worry,' said Matt. He was surprised at his own confidence. 'I won't be coming near the house again. I hope it works out for you, Laura.'

She looked at the floor again and didn't speak for a moment.

'I haven't asked about your father. Is he all right, Matt?'

'He will be,' said Matt, remembering that he had not rung to make arrangements for the weekend. 'It was a stroke. It'll slow him down but hopefully it was just a warning.'

Matt couldn't help but think that if he had not been called to Whitby, he might have gone to view the flat with Laura and she would never have got involved with Lewis. Despite himself, he felt a pang of resentment towards his father.

'I'll get going, then,' said Laura, and she stood up and moved forward. 'No hard feelings?'

'No hard feelings,' said Matt, and he did his best to smile as they made their way into the hall.

She stood back as Matt tugged at the front door and, when it finally flew open, she leaned forward and kissed him on the cheek before stepping out into the cold night.

'You need to get that fixed,' she said, softly.

'I know,' replied Matt. 'I'll see to it, I promise.'

Matt closed the door behind her. He leaned back against it, he put his head in his hands and he cried.

Chapter 20

Laura was shivering as she set off on the short drive back to Chorlton. The car heater was turned up full and it wasn't that cold anyway but Laura was shivering. She felt so depressed. She was making such a terrible mess of her life and she couldn't work out exactly why things had started to go so badly wrong.

To make matters worse, she knew she wasn't doing her job properly. The marking was stacking up and she was arriving at school later and later each morning without any proper lesson plans for the day. She was just about getting through but it wouldn't be long before Mrs Nelson picked up on her. She didn't miss much.

Perhaps it was meeting Matt that had thrown her off course, shy, polite Matt who wouldn't do anything to hurt anyone and who had seemed so vulnerable. Perhaps she should have let things take their course. No, she was right to take a step back. Matt had moved too quickly. He had expected too much.

She was right, also, to look for a place

of her own. Living with Meg and particularly Dina was becoming intolerable. The whole idea of buying a place of her own was to give herself more space, both physically and mentally. What she hadn't bargained for was meeting Lewis Jordan, suave, handsome Lewis who had breezed into her life and swept her off her feet. But now she was beginning to have doubts about Lewis. She had seen another side to him and it had both shocked her and stopped her in her tracks. Lewis was not what she thought he was.

To add to her problems, the flat she had set her heart on in Grange Road had been snapped up. Someone had stepped in with a cash offer, which had been accepted immediately. So she had no choice; she was still stuck with Meg and Dina.

Laura's mind was drifting as she drove along Barlow Moor Road towards Chorlton Bus Station. She was aware of the blue flashing lights ahead of her but it was only when she joined the queue of cars held up by the incident that the significance of the lights really registered.

'Someone else has got problems,' she muttered to herself as she braked and joined the back of the queue.

She assumed it was a traffic accident. The police had closed off one side of the road and it was slow going approaching the bus station.

Laura turned on her radio and took a deep breath as she edged slowly forward. She felt a pang of guilt as the blue lights lit up the scene ahead and a siren sounded in the distance. Someone was probably trapped in their car or lying injured in the road and she had turned on her radio to listen to some music.

'No sign of a car involved,' she muttered, as she drew nearer. 'Perhaps it's a hit and run.'

Whatever the problem, the incident was on her side of the road. It was almost directly outside the police station. The area had already been cordoned off and an ambulance was in position. A crowd of onlookers had gathered, trying to edge ever closer to the ambulance. A police officer was doing his best to keep the traffic moving but the stream of cars were creeping past, drivers lowering their windows to try and get a glimpse of the problem.

Laura couldn't resist it. As she drew level with the ambulance, she lowered her passenger window and peered out into the darkness. There, kneeling down besides a motionless figure sprawled out on the pavement, was Meg, holding on to a limp hand and whispering words of encouragement. Laura drew in her breath sharply and averted her eyes back to the road ahead. It was Meg! It was definitely Meg! She had probably got off the bus at Chorlton station and she was there to help.

Within minutes Laura had parked outside her house and returned to the scene. She pushed her way to the front of the onlookers just as the paramedics were lifting a stretcher. It was a black kid; Laura could see that much and to her distress, a limp hand flopped down from the stretcher and dangled loosely as they carried the figure into the ambulance.

'Meg!' shouted Laura. 'Meg! What's going on?'

Meg seemed dazed and disorientated. Nothing usually phased her; she was a nurse, for goodness sake. She was used to medical emergencies.

'I'm over here, Meg!'

Laura waved her hand and Meg finally realised that it was her name being called out. She looked over towards the onlookers to see someone waving at her, frantically. The blue lights from the police cars and the ambulance were still flashing and it took Meg another few moments to recognise Laura. She moved towards the crowd and, as she approached, Laura noticed the deep, dark stain on the front of her jacket.

'Laura, what are you doing here?' Meg's voice was steady but quieter than usual.

'I was driving home and I saw you with him,' explained Laura. She had reached out and taken hold of Meg's hand. 'What happened to him, Meg? Was it a hit and run?'

'Hit and run?' said Meg, shaking her head. 'He's been stabbed, Laura. Someone's stabbed him. He was there on the floor when I got off the bus.' She nodded towards a pool of blood on the pavement. 'Somebody had already found him and sent for an ambulance. Somebody's stabbed him and he's right outside the police station, for God's sake!'

'Is he going to be all right?' asked Laura. She couldn't take her eyes off the dark red pool spreading across the pavement.

'He's been stabbed, Laura. He's in a bad way.'

The doors to the ambulance closed and within seconds it pulled away, its siren screaming into the night. The police officer who seemed to be in charge took a few steps towards the crowd and shouted, 'Has anyone got any information? Did anyone see anything or can anyone identify the victim?'

'It's Linton. His name's Linton.'

The voice came from an Afro-Caribbean girl who was standing directly behind Laura. She seemed to be about fifteen years old and Laura noticed that she had braided hair. She was sobbing quietly.

'Let her through, please!' shouted the officer and Laura stood to one side as the girl squeezed past.

A female officer came across to join them almost immediately and she put a comforting arm around the girl's shoulder before leading her off towards the police station.

'Come on, let's go home,' said Laura, and she too put an arm around her friend's shoulder.

They pushed past a black youth who was standing where the girl had been and headed back across the main road towards the house.

The youth removed the cigarette he had been smoking from his mouth and flicked it onto the floor before grinding it out with his boot.

Chapter 21

Matt's dad was home. He was sitting in his favourite chair with his feet raised up on a footstool. He could see out of the window from where the chair had been positioned. He could watch the locals scurry up and down Henrietta Street, dodging the showers, pulling up their collars against the cold easterly wind.

'I've sat in this chair some times over the years,' he said, more to himself than to anyone in particular. 'Seen some comings and goings, I can tell you.'

His voice wasn't bad. It was better than Matt had expected. He had not fully regained the feeling down his left side but the voice was definitely stronger than it had been just a few days ago.

'You'll be sitting in it for a few more years yet, by the sound of things,' said Matt. 'Mum tells me the doctors are pleased with you. They must be to let you out so quickly.'

'Couldn't put up with his grumbling any longer,' said Matt's mum, as she placed a tray on a low table in the centre of the small room. 'Glad to see the back of him, I should think! A couple of days laid up and you should have heard him! Irritable old bugger!'

Matt felt disappointed when he realised that he wouldn't be seeing the young nurse again – but he was relieved at his father's progress. And his mother – she looked five years younger. She'd had her hair done and she was smiling again.

Matt's mum lifted the lid off the pot, stirred the tea and then poured out the dark brown liquid into the familiar blue mugs. Matt didn't like to tell her that he didn't take it as strong these days.

'He's going to have to do as he's told,' she said, passing a mug across to Matt. 'The doctor told him that he'd had a warning. Far less alcohol and cut out the smoking altogether from now on.' She spoke as if her husband was a child and he frowned back at her like a naughty schoolboy. 'He might not get a second chance if he doesn't behave himself.'

'Mum's right,' said Matt. 'You've got to look after yourself, Dad.'

'Don't you start!' said Matt's dad. 'I've smoked since I was fifteen. I'm sure the odd one won't make any difference at my age.'

He lowered his feet with difficulty and shuffled round in his chair. His wife leaned forward and placed the mug carefully into his hands. She had deliberately only filled it three-quarters full.

'Where's the rest of me tea?' he said, staring into the mug. 'Has somebody bloody supped it? Anyway,' he continued, turning his attention to Matt, 'you don't look as though you've been looking after yourself very well. What's up with your face? Have you been in a scrap, or something? I didn't think you had it in you, lad!'

'Not exactly a scrap,' said Matt. He felt awkward. He rubbed the dark bruise on his face gently while he searched for an explanation. 'More of a disagreement, really.'

'It's time you settled down, lad,' continued his father, and he took a sup of his tea, his hands trembling ever so slightly, his wife ready to move in and help should he falter. 'Scrapping at your age! How old are you? Thirty, is it?'

'Twenty-nine,' corrected Matt. He didn't want to talk about this.

'Me and your mother had been married for seven years by the time I was your age, lad. It's time you got yourself a woman and settled down. You're not queer, are you?'

'No, Dad, I'm not queer. Anyway, queer's acceptable these days.'

'Not to me, it isn't! I've never yet come across a queer fisherman. No time to be queer when you're out there battling against the sea. Too much else to think about.'

Matt couldn't see the logic in the argument. He couldn't see why a fisherman should be any different to a policeman or a doctor or a waiter – but he decided to keep quiet and listen. He knew he could never tell his father anything.

'Have you got yourself a girl at the moment, then?' persisted his father. 'What about that dancer you knew? What's happened to her?'

'She went to London,' answered Matt's mum. 'You know Lydia moved down to London to work years ago. Why don't you leave it, Jack?'

He was being deliberately awkward.

'Bloody tea's too hot,' he said, fumbling the mug back down onto the tray. 'Why d'you always make it so bloody hot?'

Matt glanced at his mother and smiled. He was definitely on the mend.

'Emily's on the market again,' said Matt's dad. 'Husband's left her and the little un and gone off with a barmaid from Scarborough.'

'Jack! What a terrible thing to say! You make her sound like a cow, telling our Matt she's back on the market!'

'He knows what I mean,' said her husband. He wanted a handkerchief out of his left pocket but he couldn't manage. Instead, he signalled towards a box of tissues that was on the table and his wife passed it over. 'She's available. When she lived next door, she always had a soft spot for you, Matt, right up until you went off to Manchester. Your Auntie Sarah told us that much. You missed out on that one, you did. Well, now's your chance.

Why don't you look her up while you're over here in Whitby? Once they've had it they can't do without for long, you know.'

'Jack! That's quite enough! Drink your tea and give your face a rest!'

Matt stared out to sea as he sat on the wooden bench to the side of St Mary's Church graveyard. He had realised, when he had reached the top of the one hundred and ninety-nine steps, just how unfit he had become and he was glad to sit down and recover, despite the bitter wind that carried a thin, whipping rain. Not surprisingly, he was alone. There was no one else in sight. He pulled the collar up on his coat and he stared out to sea.

He couldn't help but think that Lewis Jordan would have raced up the steps and arrived at the churchyard hardly out of breath – especially if someone was watching him. But then Lewis Jordan wouldn't visit a place such as Whitby. Not his scene at all.

Matt knew that his father had been making mischief but some of the things he said had hit home. His dad was right. He was nearly thirty years old and he still didn't know where he was going in life. He was living in a house that he had taken on under the false impression that it would become a home. He was working in a job with no prospects that had become mind-numbing in its tedious repetitiveness. He had failed miserably in the few relationships that he had had the chance to develop. Was he really that boring and undesirable that nobody wanted to stay with him for more than a few days – or a few weeks at the most, in Lydia's case? Even Beano had Dina. Perhaps he should have gone after Dina himself. Surely he couldn't have failed with Dina.

No. Matt shook his head. It didn't bear thinking about.

A gust of rain-filled wind made him shiver and he huddled further down into his coat. The sea was grey and rough and he could hear the relentless waves breaking onto the rocks below. The horizon was indistinct, a blur of sea and rain and low cloud. Some things never changed. He thought back to his childhood, when he would run up the one hundred and ninety-nine steps with Emily following behind him. He had never thought of her as anything more than a friend. On hot summer days they would go down to the beach together, play in the sand and walk along the edge of the waves. They would lose their pocket money in the noisy amusement arcades, saving just enough to buy ice creams to eat on their way back to Henrietta Street. They seemed to go on forever, those summers.

But then, suddenly, everything had changed. The *May Ellen* had gone down and life was never the same again. Auntie Sarah and Emily moved house, Emily went to a new school and visits back to Henrietta Street were few and far between. There were too many painful memories.

He'd seen her in the town sometimes, especially in their teenage years. She'd be wandering about late on a Saturday night, down by the arcade, with a big group of her new friends larking about and experimenting with cans of lager and cigarettes. Matt didn't know any of them and he didn't want to. He didn't like the look of them. He had his own group of friends. He kept out of their way.

And then he had moved to Didsbury and lost touch completely. Oh, his parents mentioned her from time to time; kept him up to date with Emily's life. 'Emily's got engaged to David. He's such a nice young man.' 'Emily's getting married in August.' 'Emily and David have bought themselves a little house at Sandsend.' 'Emily's had a baby girl. She's called her Gina. Not too keen on the name but she's such a sweet little thing.'

Well. Emily was *on the market* again, as his father so tactfully put it and Matt couldn't help but wonder what she was like. How had the years treated her? What would she look like? Did she ever think of their childhood days together? Did she ever give him a second thought? He wondered for a moment whether or not he should contact her. He had the opportunity. He was over in Whitby. A sudden gust of wind made him clutch at his collar and he dismissed the idea as ridiculous.

Matt's father was right – he needed to do something with his life. Suddenly, the thought of returning to Number 32 Ashton Avenue, East Didsbury, filled him with depression. He could picture himself walking up to the faded front door and turning the key, pushing against the door because he hadn't bothered to get it fixed, entering the dark hallway that was beginning to smell more musty with each week that passed. He didn't want to keep going back to the fitted kitchen shop in Chorlton. He didn't want to listen to Beano talking about his adventures with Dina – if he had any breath left to talk. He wanted something different.

And then there was Laura. It was over. He had finally accepted that it was over and he couldn't bear the thought of bumping into her and Lewis in Didsbury as he plodded on with his monotonous existence.

It was the obvious thing to do – he would turn his back on his boring, mediocre life and start again in Whitby. And yes, he could even look up Emily and, if the goods were in order, he could dabble in the market.

Matt had made up his mind. As he sat there in the cold, Whitby wind, overlooking the grey harbour, the rain soaking through his clothes, he had decided that even this was preferable to his wasted life in Didsbury.

He would return to Ashton Avenue and put the property up for sale. He had to smile. There was certainly one estate agent he wouldn't be approaching with his business!

Chapter 22

Laura didn't want to go.

She had met a few of Lewis' friends when they had gathered for a drink together in The Old Cock and she had been less than favourably impressed. She had met Richard, Jason and Dougie, friends from Lewis' university days who had been with him on the P.E. course and had been members of the rugby team. They looked and acted like rugby players, or rather ex-rugby players. They were overweight and horrendously loud. They talked non-stop for most of the evening about the great times they'd experienced together – drinking binges, girls and silly pranks they'd played on each other. Laura sat and listened and smiled at the right places, more in relief that she hadn't been at uni with them.

Dougie was the loudest. He had a shock of untidy ginger hair that escaped from his head in all directions. He'd say something that wasn't in the least bit funny and then roar with laughter, so that everyone else had to join in to avoid embarrassment.

Jason gave her the creeps. He kept staring at her blouse, his light blue eyes unblinking and gradually widening. He'd sip his pint, lick his lips and then stare again, long and hard, until someone nudged him or brought him into the conversation. Laura felt uncomfortable. She was glad she wasn't sitting next to him. She could imagine him putting his hand on her leg under the table and she made a mental note to keep her distance.

Richard was OK. He was tall and good looking and had definitely kept himself in better shape than the others, Lewis excepted. Richard had obviously done well for himself since graduating and he made sure everyone knew. He had become a partner with a media company based in Manchester, concentrating on advertising and PR. Laura heard all about his luxury apartment at Salford Quays, about his frequent foreign holidays and about his top of the range Land Rover.

'I'll give you a ride in it, sometime,' he had promised, when Lewis was at the bar ordering a round of drinks. 'You can come and see the apartment. I think you'd be impressed.'

Laura doubted it very much but she said nothing.

And then there was Paula and her dreadful friend Clarissa. They breezed into the pub, all short skirts, tight jumpers and supported breasts, making absolutely sure that everyone noticed them as they approached the rugby corner. It had been a signal for Dougie to turn up the decibels even more, which seemed to please the girls as it attracted further attention their way. Jason had shuffled round and guided Clarissa into the vacant space. His eyes had visibly widened and Laura's blouse was suddenly no longer interesting. Laura was sure he was salivating. He kept rubbing his mouth with the back of his hand. Laura couldn't help but notice that the same hand was on Clarissa's leg within ten minutes. Still, she didn't seem to mind.

Paula had strutted straight up to Lewis, taken his head in both her hands and kissed him, loudly. Lewis had made a space for her to sit next to him, nudging Laura further along the seat, and then he had announced brusquely: 'Paula, I'd like you to meet Laura. She's a primary school teacher. I don't think you know each other.'

He couldn't have made her sound more boring if he had yawned.

The smile disappeared from Paula's face. She leaned forward and stared at Laura, as if she was a slightly suspect dress in a shop window and, after a few seconds, she said, 'Hi, Laura. Pleased to meet you. A primary school teacher? That's great! We'll have a chat about that later. In the meantime, there's a few things you need to know about Lewis.'

'She'll have discovered a few things for herself by now,' shouted Dougie, so loud that the whole pub could hear, and he rocked back in his seat and bellowed with laughter.

Laura smiled, uncomfortably. She just knew it was going to be a long evening.

'What do you mean you don't want to go?' Lewis put the key in the ignition and clicked on his seat belt. 'Dougie throws a great party. You know what a good laugh he is – and you'll know other people there. You've met some of them already.'

'I just thought we were going out on our own,' said Laura. 'That's what we arranged. A quiet meal on a Saturday night. I thought we could go to the Italian. You didn't say anything about a party, Lewis.'

'I didn't *know* anything about a party,' explained Lewis. 'It's short notice. Dougie only rang me this morning. That's what he's like. That's the way we all operate – on the spur of the moment.'

'But I'm tired, Lewis. I told you, I'm having a hard time at work. I'm not coping.'

'All the more reason to switch off and relax,' said Lewis. He turned the key in the ignition and the Audi roared into life. 'I tell you, Dougie throws a great party. Trust me – we'll have a good time.'

Dougie lived in Cheadle Hulme. He owned his own house, a large, red-bricked semi with a wide gravel driveway. Laura immediately felt sorry for the neighbours. They were bound to be able to hear Dougie's voice no matter how thick the walls were. Lewis had parked in the road, half on and half off the pavement and Laura could hear the monotonous base thump of the music as soon as she stepped out of the car. She hated that sort of music. It gave her a headache. She always associated it with open car windows and baseball hats worn back to front. They walked up the gravel path towards the front door, Lewis clutching hold of a large bottle of vodka.

'Don't look so apprehensive,' he said, taking hold of Laura's arm. 'Lighten up a bit, will you!'

Laura gave a weak smile and followed him through the open doorway. There was Dougie, straight in front of them, hair a mess, glass of beer in one hand, cigarette in the other. It was only half past nine and he already looked dishevelled and unsteady.

'Lew-is!' he bellowed, and he raised his arms, spilling his beer. 'Lew-is and Laur-en! What kept you?' He tottered towards them. 'I was beginning to think you'd had a better offer!'

'Doug-ie!' responded Lewis, approaching his friend and throwing a mock punch. 'As if anyone could give me a better offer than you!' Lewis thrust the bottle of vodka forward and Dougie indicated towards the kitchen.

'Put it in there, will you mate. And get yourself and Lauren a drink!' he guffawed and coughed and then stumbled off towards the incessant, thumping base noise.

Lewis headed for the kitchen and Laura followed him. She couldn't understand why the place was so crowded. Other parties she'd been to hadn't got going until after the pubs were shut.

It was a large kitchen, badly lit by a strip light that flickered and stuttered constantly. Laura stood at the door and peered in at the light oak units, neat but slightly dated. They were the same units her mother had changed six years ago. There was a group of people gathered near the back door, clutching glasses and cigarettes, several of them talking at once. Laura didn't recognise any of them. One or two others had already spilled out into the back garden, even though it was damp and miserable. The kitchen work surfaces were cluttered with glasses, cans and bottles. Lewis could just about find a space to deposit his vodka. He pushed it in amongst the beer and wine bottles and then turned towards the group.

'Steve!' he said, placing his hand on the nearest shoulder. 'How's it going? And Jess! Long time no see!'

'Look who's here!' responded Steve, shaking Lewis by the hand. 'Thought you'd disappeared! Been abducted by aliens, or something! What have you been doing with yourself?'

'Oh, this and that,' said Lewis, and he moved forward so that he was absorbed into the group. Someone thrust a bottle of beer into his hand and he took a long swig that almost half emptied it.

Laura felt awkward. She didn't know whether to move in and join him or stay put in the hope that Lewis would turn back to her. She was still trying to make a decision when Dougie trundled up behind her. His glass was empty and he was obviously ready for a refill.

'Lauren!' he gushed. 'You're looking gorgeous! Has that stupid bastard deserted you already? Somebody should have warned you about him! Don't just stand there – get yourself a drink! Help yourself, lass, there's plenty to choose from. And then come and join us next door.' He indicated towards the room with the thumping music. 'That's where it's all happening, you know. Not in here with these miserable sods! The girls are next door. Bring your drink through.'

Laura smiled, more in embarrassment than politeness. She poured herself a glass of Chianti and then hesitated before approaching Lewis. He was listening to some involved tale that Steve was relating. Steve looked a few years older than Lewis, a big man with short-cropped fair hair and a protruding nose that had obviously been broken at some point in his life. Laura guessed that he was probably another of Lewis' rugby chums who had given up years ago and had gone to seed. He might have given up the game but he had clearly not given up the drink; he punctuated his story with great slurps of beer taken directly from the bottle, wiping his mouth with the back of his hand after every gulp.

Laura wasn't sure if Jess, the feeble woman by Steve's side, was his wife or girlfriend. She looked as though she hadn't seen the sun for years. Her skin was the colour of overcooked cold pasta. Her pale, languid face with its droopy eyelids showed no hint of expression whatsoever. Laura had always thought the rugby boys went for big, loud buxom wenches. Something had clearly gone badly wrong in this case.

Laura stared hard at Jess for a few moments and then she decided. She took hold of Lewis' arm to attract his attention and when he turned to glance at her she said, 'Are you coming through, Lewis? The girls are in the other room.'

'Brilliant!' said Lewis. 'You go ahead and have a chat with them. I'll be with you in a few minutes, as soon as Steve has finished.' And he shook her hand from his arm and turned back towards the big man, who burped as he wiped away the traces of another swig of beer with the back of his hand. Laura stared at Lewis' back for a few moments before turning and heading for the music, pausing briefly to take a sip of her

Chianti.

She entered the lounge and took in the scene with a glance. The first thing she noticed was the blue light. Dougie had removed the three light bulbs from their holder in the centre of the ceiling and replaced them with low wattage blue bulbs that cast a stunted glow and made the room's occupants look ill. The furniture was sparse, consisting of a long, beige leather sofa against the back wall, one matching chair and an oblong, smoked glass coffee table. A large flat screen TV stood on its own stand in the corner of the room, opposite the sofa. There was a badly framed print of a scrum of rugby players on the wall above the gas fire and there was an equally badly framed print of Van Gogh's *Sunflowers* above the couch. That was bad taste. They didn't go together. All this in a glance, accompanied by the steady, base thump that seemed to be striving to escape from an incredibly small iPod and speaker dock.

And then there were the people – the awful people, some of whom she recognised immediately. There was Jason, sitting at the far end of the sofa, his arm loosely around the shoulder of a girl she hadn't seen before. The girl seemed much younger than Jason, dark haired, fresh faced, maybe a first year university student. She was smoking, or rather holding a cigarette in her hand and her friend, who had viciously short-cropped blonde hair, was perched on the arm of the sofa.

The blonde girl was obviously in the middle of delivering an incredibly long and complicated tale and Laura watched as Jason's hand crept further over the dark haired girl's shoulder, towards the front of her blouse.

Paula and Clarissa were over towards the TV, drinks in hands, chatting with two other young women of about the same age. One of them was an Asian girl, tall and slender and classically good-looking. The other was what Laura referred to as 'a crowd scene' – someone who went through life looking like a thousand others; someone you wouldn't recognise if you bumped into her a day later. Laura had always thought of herself as a bit of a crowd scene. Paula had noticed Laura the moment she had entered the room but had deliberately avoided eye contact. Laura didn't like her. There was such an arrogance about her, a loud arrogance that seemed to set her apart from everybody else in the room. Clarissa waved weakly but gave no signal for Laura to join them. She simply turned her attention back to her friends and drew more deeply on her cigarette. There was already a haze of cigarette smoke in the room and Laura instinctively rubbed her eyes. She wished she was somewhere else, anywhere else but this awful house.

It was dreadful. Laura had stopped feeling awkward and embarrassed and, instead, was feeling angry. How dare Lewis bring her here, deposit her amongst these aliens, especially when he knew it was the last thing she wanted. How dare he stay drinking in the kitchen, leaving her isolated and alone. The music thumped out in anger and she began to relate to it. She drank more Chianti.

The doorbell sounded and a new cluster of aliens tumbled into the hall, to be greeted by Dougie's thunderous voice.

'Kev-in! And Belind-a! How are you? And Frank-ie! Long time no see! Oh – you shouldn't have bothered! Put them through there, will you folks. And sort yourselves out with drinks!'

Laura looked at her empty glass and decided that she needed another drink herself. And she needed Lewis. She was marooned amidst the aliens, who were completely ignoring her, and she needed Lewis to rescue her. She made up her mind and walked decisively back towards the kitchen, just as Jason's fingers progressed a few more centimetres down the front of the dark haired girl's blouse.

The kitchen was noisy and crowded. The new arrivals were blocking the doorway and Laura had to push her way through. She couldn't see Lewis, or Steve, for that matter. They weren't over by the door where she'd left them deep in irrelevant conversation. She poured herself another large glass of red wine to buy herself time to think. The Chianti was finished but Laura didn't really care what she was drinking. The heady mix of red wine together with the constant, thumping music and the confusion of voices was already beginning to take its effect. She took a large gulp from the over full glass and turned, to be faced by Dougie, looking even more dishevelled and unstable. His face was blotched red and he was sweating profusely. A limp cigarette hung loosely from his lips, the rising smoke causing him to squint and screw up his eyes.

'How's it going?' Dougie stammered. 'Everything all right, is it?'

He seemed to lean to one side and Laura thought he was about to fall over.

'Everything's fine,' she lied, and she was aware that her own voice was beginning to sound slightly slurred. 'You haven't seen Lewis, have you?'

She wafted the drifting smoke away from her face.

'He's just slipped out with Steve and a couple of the lads,' said Dougie. 'Down to the local for a few quick ones. They'll be back, don't worry. The night's still young.' Even in his state he must have noticed the look on Laura's face and he added, 'It's not a problem, is it, Lauren?'

'It's Laura!' snapped Laura. 'And no – it's not a problem. Nothing I can't handle, anyway.'

She pushed past him and headed back towards the front room, where the steady, moronic beat seemed to be booming louder and louder. Laura took a large gulp of red wine, a deep breath and then re-entered the arena.

Chapter 23

Linton's father was a sorry figure sitting by his son's side in the Intensive Care Unit. The phone call had hit him like a bullet but, in a strange sort of way, he wasn't surprised; he had almost been expecting the call. His first thought had been to let Linton's mother know what had happened but he wasn't sure where she was – somewhere in Birmingham the last time he had heard from her. A neighbour had agreed to look after Melissa as soon as news of the stabbing broke and now, as he sat holding his son's motionless hand, he could not avoid a feeling of intense guilt and self-blame.

Where had it all gone wrong? He could look back in his mind and picture Linton as a happy, carefree boy of nine or ten with a permanent grin on his face; he could see him in his crisp, new uniform the day he started high school, he could picture him turning and waving at his mother as he walked off down the path; he could still sense the pride the day Linton was awarded the Sports Prize at the end of his first school year – and then the family had broken up and the smile had disappeared from Linton's face. He knew he was as much to blame for the split as his wife. He was stubborn and he was authoritarian and he was seldom willing to listen to anyone, let alone his wife. And where had it led him? To a hospital bed where his son was being fed by drips and could only breathe with the aid of an oxygen mask.

A voice interrupted his thoughts and made him jump momentarily.

'Mr Hill? I'm sorry to intrude. I'm Doctor Banister. This is a difficult time for you.'

'Very difficult,' agreed Linton's father. 'It's a very difficult time.'

'I appreciate what you're going through,' continued the doctor, pulling up a chair, 'and you'll have our full support, I assure you.'

'Well, thank you for that,' said Linton's father, and he added: 'Is he going to be all right?'

'It's early days yet,' and he paused to give the question full thought, 'but I think he's going to be all right. It was a vicious blow, mind you. The knife entered his chest with such force that it broke two of his ribs and punctured his lung. He's been a lucky boy.'

'Lucky?' repeated Linton's father. 'You call it lucky being stabbed in the chest and put in an Intensive Care Unit?'

'He could have been killed. He's alive and he should make a good recovery,' said the doctor, quietly. 'He's been given a second chance, make sure he doesn't waste it!'

'I'm sorry, doctor. As you said, it's very difficult at the moment.'

'It's times like these that make you realise just how fragile life can be,' said Doctor Banister. 'Take care, Mr Hill.'

And he turned and walked away, just as Linton's eyes flickered slowly open and focused on a thin crack that snaked across the ceiling above him.

Chapter 24

It was just turning eleven-thirty and Matt was coming to the end of yet another boring Saturday evening. Earlier, he had thought about taking a walk down to The Old Cock. There was always a chance that he would bump into someone he knew but somehow the hours had just drifted on and by the time he had finally reached a decision he realised it was too late. He had been visiting The Old Cock less and less lately, especially as Beano never seemed to be available. Instead, this Saturday evening he had settled down with a bottle of beer to watch the football highlights. Matt's team had lost. Leeds United were in trouble and he could relate to their decline.

A great deal had happened since his return from Whitby ten days ago. Matt had visited Johnson's Estate Agents on Monday lunchtime and, having explained that he wished to put his house up for sale, a valuation was arranged for that same evening. That had sent Matt into immediate panic. The place was filthy. It would take two weeks to make it look anything like respectable.

Matt had finished work an hour early and called in at the supermarket to stock up on cleaning materials and air fresheners. He'd started with the kitchen as that was the biggest disaster area. The floor was easy enough to mop but the oven and the cooker hob were a real challenge. And how did all those grease marks get on the ceiling? That was strange. He had it looking passable within an hour – it just looked as if it needed a good clean – and then he moved on to the bathroom.

That was more of a puzzle. How on earth could it look like that with only one person using it? You stood in the shower, sprayed yourself with hot water, worked up a good foam with the shower gel and shampoo and yet the booth looked as if it had been sprayed with fertilizer by an over-zealous farmer.

The plug-hole worried him most. Matt had been aware for some time that the water was taking longer than it should to drain away and when he got down on his knees and inspected the plug hole he realised why. Where had all that hair come from? If it had come from his head he was in trouble. He'd be bald within five years. He peered at his hair through the film on the bathroom mirror and, although it was thinning slightly, he was reasonably reassured. Matt gave up on the bathroom after forty-five minutes, having convinced himself that the estate agent was unlikely to want to take a shower or peer down the toilet.

The rest of the house was dealt with less thoroughly – more tidying and clearing away than cleaning. Matt had not got a linen basket so the dirty washing that littered his bedroom floor, including seven pairs of used boxer shorts, was shoved quickly inside his wardrobe. There was quite a pile of it and it took some effort to close the door – but he succeeded and he was satisfied that the bedroom looked acceptable.

The estate agent was due at seven-thirty and he arrived five minutes early. Matt opened the front door, with some difficulty, to be greeted by a man in his late twenties or early thirties, rather thin with vivid ginger hair and brown-rimmed glasses. He wore a brown two piece suit to complement his hair. It didn't work.

'James Johnson,' he announced, thrusting a hand forward, clipboard under his other arm. 'I'm the *and Son* from Johnson and Son.'

'Pleased to meet you,' lied Matt. 'Come on in.'

'Just a hint for you,' said James Johnson, stepping into the hallway, 'you could do with getting that door fixed. First impressions and all that.'

'Thanks – I'll see to it,' said Matt, taking an instant dislike to yet another estate agent. First impressions and all that.

From the moment James Johnson entered

the hallway his eyes were everywhere and the look on his face told Matt instantly that he was not impressed.

'Do you mind me asking how long you've lived here?' said James Johnson, as Matt struggled to push the door closed.

'I've had it for five years,' said Matt. 'I appreciate it needs a bit of attention – but you know what it's like when you live on your own. You don't tend to bother the same, do you?'

'Obviously not,' said James Johnson, and he made his first scrawled notes on a pad that he had flicked open. 'Still, you can rest assured that Johnson's Estate Agents will offer you a first class service – whatever the state your property's in.'

The rest of the evaluation continued in the same mode – plenty of suggestions and the atmosphere growing colder by the minute. By the time the selling price was agreed and James Johnson stepped back into the street, Matt was thoroughly depressed.

'I'll never sell it,' he said out loud. 'I don't know why I bothered!'

Four days later the house was sold. Matt didn't meet the buyer – Mr George, a fifty-something business man who dabbled in property and apparently owned several other houses in the Didsbury area. James Johnson had arranged the viewing when Matt was at work and the first Matt knew about it was when he took a call on his mobile.

'He's offered you eight thousand less than the asking price,' explained James Johnson. 'He says he'll have to rip everything out and completely redecorate if he's to stand a chance of letting it. And I'm sorry to say he did look inside a few of your cupboards. I've left your boxer shorts on the bedroom floor where they dropped out.'

Matt closed his eyes and winced. He'd meant to put them in the washing machine. He'd worn the same pair for the last three days.

'Tell him I'll meet him half way,' said Matt, ignoring the comment about his boxer shorts. 'Tell him I'll drop by four thousand and see what he says.'

In the end, Matt dropped by five thousand. James Johnson advised him to hang on, to wait and see what other offers came in, but Matt wanted rid. He'd had enough of Didsbury and he was ready to sort out his life. So Mr George it was. There was no chain involved in the sale and early completion was expected. Matt already had a flat lined up above a chemist's shop in Whitby. There was no way he could go back to living with his parents in Henrietta Street. They were all right to visit once in a while but his father would drive him mad. The flat wasn't brilliant accommodation but it was cheap to rent and it would serve the purpose until he could find something more permanent.

And now, just after eleven-thirty on this

Saturday evening, Matt couldn't resist opening his front door and taking yet another look at the *SOLD* sign that stood out in bold purple from the side of his house. He stared at it for a few moments through the steady drizzle that had begun to fall and a surge of satisfaction surfaced – tempered by just a tinge of regret at the thought of what might have been.

Matt closed the door, pleased that he had finally organised a joiner, who had taken only minutes to sort it out. He collected a glass of water from the kitchen and switched on the washing machine before ascending the stairs for yet another early night. Tomorrow would be a new day – and he'd even have clean boxer shorts to celebrate its dawn.

Chapter 25

Laura had drunk far too much. She was slouched back on the sofa, clutching a half empty glass of red wine, pretending to listen to the cropped blonde, who had hardly taken a breath for ten minutes. Jason had long since disappeared upstairs with the dark haired girl. The room had filled up and the noise was making Laura's head spin, the chatter and laughter getting louder and louder in an effort to combat the incessant, throbbing music.

It was just past midnight and Lewis had still not returned. Laura had almost forgotten about him. Her eyes were glazing over and her mind was swimming with confused images. One moment she was at school, in the classroom watching George chewing his pencil and glaring at a strange man that had just entered and was standing by the door. And then she was in the playground listening to Matt screaming at her through the mesh fencing; she saw herself in The Old Cock, listening to Richard and Jason and Dougie bragging about their rugby exploits, with Paula and the dreadful Clarissa drooling over their every word. Surprisingly, Matt was there, too, in her mixed up mind, sitting quietly in the background sipping a Southern Comfort. Why was Matt there? Why did he keep drifting in and out of her confused visions? She couldn't get him out of her mind and she didn't know why. And then Dougie's blotched face leered in front of her and his slurred voice shook her out of her visionary ramblings. He was there, really there, spilling his drink over her as he put out a hand to shake her shoulder.

'I thought you'd like to know Lewis is back,' he stammered. 'He's in the kitchen, Lauren. You want to go through and see him?'

Laura's eyes widened and she shook her head. 'Yes, yes – thanks,' she said. 'I'll be through in a minute.'

'That was in Ibiza,' the blonde girl was saying. 'We had a great time – what I can remember of it! You ever been to Ibiza? Wicked!'

'Wh-what? No, no! Not really my type of place,' said Laura, leaning forward unsteadily.

She felt terrible. The red wine had taken its effect and Laura's head was pounding in time with the music. The room was thick with smoke, a strange smelling haze hung in the air and added to her dizziness. She tried to stand up but fell back on the sofa again. She was hot and the other people in the room were blurred and confused. She felt most peculiar. Laura tried again and this time she was more successful. She stood still for a moment and took a deep breath as gradually, the figures came more into focus.

'You want to give it a try,' insisted the blonde girl. 'I'm sure you'd like it. Totally pissed every night. And the men . . .'

'Yes, thanks,' said Laura, unconvincingly. 'I might do that. Thanks . . .'

She focused on the door and moved forward, slowly at first, but then more confidently. The house had become even more crowded and Laura pushed her way past a group standing in the hallway, so that she could reach the kitchen door. Lewis was there, with Steve, over near the fridge chatting and laughing with two girls she had never set eyes on before, arms draped around their shoulders. Laura just stood in the doorway and stared, the anger welling up inside.

Steve saw her first and her face must have said everything. He nudged Lewis and indicated in Laura's direction.

'Laura!' drawled Lewis, removing his arm from around the girl's shoulder and taking a long drag on his cigarette. 'How's it going? You enjoying the party? Come over and meet Suzie and, er . . .' He dragged on his cigarette and wobbled unsteadily.

'Where have you been?' said Laura, moving into the kitchen. The words were surprisingly clear and controlled. 'You've left me on my own for hours.'

'On your own?' repeated Lewis, through a haze of cigarette smoke. 'How could you be on your own at Dougie's? I told you it would be a good do!'

'I want to leave,' said Laura, steadily. 'I want to leave now. Will you take me home, Lewis?'

'Of course you don't want to leave,' said Lewis, reaching for a bottle of wine. 'No one leaves Dougie's at this time. Relax. Have another drink. The night's only just getting going.'

The two girls nudged each other and giggled. Steve smirked and took another swig of beer.

Lewis spilled some wine into a tumbler and thrust it towards Laura.

'I don't want more wine,' said Laura, taking a step backwards. 'I want to go home, Lewis. I want to go now.'

'Don't be stupid,' insisted Lewis. 'You'll feel better after another drink.' He stumbled forward and the tumbler lurched towards Laura, its contents spilling onto the front of her blouse.

'Lewis!' she screamed, and she lashed out and knocked the glass from his hand, sending it crashing to the kitchen floor where it shattered into pieces.

There was a moment's silence before it was broken by Lewis.

'Stupid bitch! What was that for?'

The kitchen was deathly quiet again and even the steady, bass thump of the moronic music seemed somewhere at the back of Laura's mind.

'What was that for?' repeated Lewis, wobbling unsteadily. 'What's your fucking problem?'

'Bastard!' yelled Laura, taking a step backwards. 'You selfish bastard, Lewis!' And she turned and barged past the people crowded into the hallway, knocking them into each other, sending several more drinks tumbling to the floor.

The front door was open and Laura stumbled out into the cold night air. It was raining and the cold and the damp hit her, making her gasp with shock. She was running, running down the drive and through the gate and into the road. She ran past Lewis' black Audi and then she heard his voice yelling her name from somewhere behind but she didn't stop to glance back, she ran on and on into the night. Breathless, she slowed to walking pace, shivering in the steady rain. She stepped into the road as a couple returning from a night out passed her, collars turned up for protection against the dampness, staring suspiciously as she gulped in the cold night air. Car headlights loomed suddenly and she jumped back onto the pavement as a taxi raced past, drenching her legs with a shower of spray.

Laura didn't know where she was. It was

past midnight and she was wandering around Cheadle Hulme with no money and no idea what to do next. Her head was still swimming from the effects of the red wine and the intoxicating haze that had filled Dougie's front room. She stopped for a moment and looked around in despair. She suddenly realised that tears were streaming down her face and she wiped them away with the back of her hand. And then a voice behind her made her jump and she turned to face the couple who had passed a few moments earlier.

'Are you all right, luv'? You look as though you're struggling a bit?

They were younger than Laura and it was the man who had spoken.

Laura stood there, shivering, glancing from one face to the other.

'Leave her alone,' urged the girl, 'she's on something.'

'Are you all right?' repeated the man. 'What's happened to you?'

'I'm all right . . .' began Laura, her voice trembling with emotion. 'It's just my boyfriend . . . we were at this party . . .'

She didn't get any further. There was a scream of wheels and a blaze of headlights as Lewis' black Audi screeched to a halt next to them. The driver's door opened and Lewis jumped out and rested his elbows on top of the car.

'Laura – get in.' His eyes were wide and

his breath turned to steam in the cold night air.

She didn't move. She stared from Lewis to the young couple and then back to Lewis.

'Get in!' he repeated. 'You've nowhere to go. How are you going to get home?'

'We'll see she's all right,' began the stranger. 'It's not a . . .'

He was cut short as Lewis exploded. 'Piss off!' he screamed, and he banged his fists on the car roof. 'Piss off, now! It's none of your fucking business!'

The couple backed away quickly and disappeared into the drizzle.

'Look, I'm sorry,' said Lewis, taking a deep breath. 'I was out of order, OK? Just get in the car and I'll take you back to Dougie's place. It's not a problem, OK?'

Laura took a step backwards and stared at him in disbelief. She shook her head slowly. 'You really don't understand do you, Lewis? I'm not going back to Dougie's place. I can't stand him! I can't stand any of them, Lewis!'

There was a moment's pause. Lewis lowered his eyes to the rain soaked ground and then, before Laura knew what was happening, he shot round the front of the car and grabbed hold of her arm.

'Lewis!' she screamed. 'You're hurting me, Lewis! I'm not going . . .'

Lewis wrenched open the passenger door

and forced Laura down into the seat. He slammed the door closed and returned to the driver's side. Laura had slumped forward and she was holding her head in her hands, the tears streaming again. Lewis revved hard and the engine roared into life. The headlights cut through the rain and the car lurched forward.

Laura sat back and gripped the side of the seat as the black Audi tore into the night, its wheels spinning and screaming. Lewis veered across the road, correcting just in time, avoiding smashing into a blue van by a whisker. He was breathing heavily and his eyes were wide, staring straight ahead, unblinkingly into the windscreen. He leaned forward over the wheel, oblivious to the fact that his wipers weren't switched on, oblivious to Laura pleading with him to slow down.

'Lewis!' she screamed, 'Lewis! Stop the car . . . please stop the car!'

Lewis took no notice. His eyes were fixed to the road ahead. If anything, he revved harder so that the sheer speed he was travelling cleared the rain from the windscreen, leaving a smeared view of the road ahead. Laura saw a drunk stagger from the pavement and she screamed as he froze like a rabbit in the beam of the headlights. He swayed back at the very last moment, crashing down into the gutter as Lewis thumped his fist into the middle of the steering wheel, causing the horn to blare out its warning.

'Lewis – please!' Laura's voice was frantic with panic.

'Stupid bitch!' Lewis seemed to spit the words out. 'Stupid fucking bitch – in front of my friends!'

'I didn't want to come!' screamed Laura. 'You know I didn't want to come!'

The road narrowed and there was a sharp bend to the left. Lewis wrenched the steering wheel down and the car screamed and skidded as it tried to adjust. Laura screamed with it. There was a bridge directly ahead, a railway bridge that went over the road. They had to pass beneath but there were headlights coming the other way. There were headlights coming towards them through the rain and they were too far over; the lights were too far over and Lewis was heading straight towards them. He realised at the last moment and he pulled the wheel down to the left, causing the car to veer and scream again. The front wing clipped the bridge wall with a sickening metallic crunch and a hail of sparks. The Audi spun across the wet surface and crashed full force into the opposite wall of the bridge, hurling metallic fragments and glass into the air as if blasted by a bomb. The oncoming car braked too late and thudded into what was left of the back section of the Audi, sending it spinning again until it grated to a halt beneath the shattered bridge, where it smouldered and steamed in deathly silence.

Chapter 26

The phone call came at 2.00 a.m. Matt couldn't work out what it was at first. He lay there in the dark, completely disorientated as the tone droned on relentlessly, somewhere in the distance. Why didn't the noise stop? Why didn't somebody do something about it? And then, in an awful moment of recognition, he realised that it was his own phone ringing downstairs. He immediately thought of his father and he panicked. Something had happened. He'd had another stroke. Phone calls in the night always brought bad news. Matt threw the covers to one side and snapped on the bedside lamp. The phone was still ringing. Someone needed to speak to him. He stumbled towards the bedroom door and pulled it open. The phone sounded so loud in the silent house. He was downstairs in seconds and the phone was in his hand. He held his breath as he answered it.

'Matt, it's Meg here. I'm at the hospital. There's been an accident.'

Matt was confused. It was not what he expected. Meg didn't know his father.

'What do you mean *an accident*?'

'Matt, it's Laura. There's been a car crash. They brought her in about twenty minutes ago.'

'A car crash?' Matt repeated the words and then shook his head in disbelief. 'Laura's been in a car crash?'

'She was with Lewis,' said Meg, quietly. 'He was driving the car and he hit a wall.'

'Is she . . . what's happened to her?'

'I only saw her for a few minutes,' explained Meg. 'She was alive but she was in a mess.'

Matt felt sick. He sank down onto a chair, the phone still clasped to his ear. He didn't speak for a few moments and Meg broke the silence.

'Are you still there, Matt? Are you all right? I thought you'd want to know.'

'Yes, thanks Meg. I'm coming in. I'm on my way.'

Matt put the phone down and sat still in the dark. Meg's words were echoing in his head and he was desperately trying to make sense of them. *A car crash – hit a wall – she's in a mess.* And then he pulled himself together. 'You've got to hold on, Laura.' He said the words out loud. 'You've got to hold on.'

Meg was waiting for him when he arrived at the hospital. Too upset to work, she had been released from duty and she was waiting just inside the main entrance. He saw her standing there as the double doors opened automatically and he rushed towards her.

'What happened?' he asked. The words were clear but he was churning inside. 'Where is she, Meg?'

'She's in theatre. She's going to be all right, Matt.'

'Are you sure? How do you know she's going to be all right?'

'She's in a bad way but the doctors have said she's going to be all right. She's not in danger.'

'Will I be able to see her? When she comes out of theatre, I mean?'

'Not for a while, Matt. I've rung her family, of course. They'll want to see her first.'

'Yes, of course,' said Matt, and he realised for the first time that he was shaking. 'Of course they'll want to see her first.'

Meg took hold of his arm and guided him away from the entrance. 'Come and get a cup of tea,' she said. 'If you want to stay for a while there's somewhere we can wait. We should get some news when she comes out of theatre.'

Matt allowed himself to be led forward like a child. His mind, although confused, was racing. He realised that he didn't know Laura's family and he wondered what he would say to them. He didn't really want to meet them – not under these circumstances. He had so many questions to ask and he didn't know where to begin.

'What did she . . . look like?' he said, slowly. The words were painful and his eyes betrayed his fear.

'Matt, I've seen so many people who've been in traffic accidents,' said Meg, gently. 'She's cut and she's battered and she's bruised. They always look a mess when they're first brought in but she'll come through it, Matt. It's the mental scars that'll take longer to heal.'

'You said she was with Lewis?' said Matt, and his voice hardened. 'I guess he was driving. What sort of a state is he in?' He was asking out of curiosity rather than concern.

'He's dead, Matt. They got him in the ambulance but he died on the way here. Laura doesn't know yet.'

Matt nodded his head slowly. He felt neither sorrow nor satisfaction, just a numbing coldness that sent a violent shiver through his whole body.

Matt jumped up with a start when he heard a voice speaking his name.

'Mr Hudson? If you want to come through you can see her now.'

He had stretched out across three chairs

in a small, private waiting room, eventually drifting into a fitful, uneasy sleep through sheer exhaustion. Meg had left him at about three in the morning. The news had come through that Laura was out of theatre and that her parents were at her bedside. 'As comfortable as can be expected' was the most that Matt got at first, but Meg was able to confirm that things had gone well in theatre. Matt had refused to leave the hospital and Meg had taken him to the stark waiting room.

'How is she?' asked Matt. He looked a mess. His hair was sticking up and his clothes were dishevelled.

'She's doing OK,' replied the nurse, holding open the waiting room door. 'You can only stay a few minutes. She's on a ventilator. She had a collapsed lung, amongst other things but she's doing OK. All being well she'll be out of Intensive Care pretty quickly. Don't be put off by all the tubes.'

'Intensive Care?' repeated Matt. 'She's in Intensive Care?'

'It's the best place for her,' explained the nurse. 'You want what's best for her, don't you?'

'She's in Intensive Care,' repeated Matt, ignoring the question. 'It can't be good if she's in Intensive Care.'

The nurse didn't reply. Instead, she led him along a short corridor before turning right into the Intensive Care Unit.

'You've got her to yourself for a few minutes,' explained the nurse. 'Her parents have gone for a cup of tea.'

She indicated towards a bed in the corner and Matt moved forward, slowly. Laura was lying on her back, eyes closed. Matt stood at the side of her bed. He didn't say anything at first. He hardly recognised her. This wasn't the Laura he knew; the Laura he had loved to wake up next to in the morning and stare at while she still lay sleeping. Now he stared down at her bruised and swollen face and he swallowed hard as the tears welled in his eyes. A diagonal gash across her forehead had been stitched and it disappeared into her hairline. An array of machines and equipment stood to the left of the bed and there were tubes leading from the machines into her nose. A saline drip fed into her right arm.

Matt leaned forward. He didn't know what to say. He spoke her name quietly.

'Laura. Can you hear me, Laura? It's Matt.'

Her eyelids flickered but they didn't open. He tried again.

'Laura – it's all right. Everything's going to be OK.'

This time her eyes opened slowly and she focused on his face bending over her. He took hold of her hand, which was resting outside the bedclothes, and he pressed it gently. He wasn't sure that she recognised him.

'Everything's going to be all right,' he repeated. 'You're going to be OK.'

She couldn't have answered even if she wanted to but, as he stood there, leaning over her, two single tears began to trickle slowly down her bruised cheeks.

Chapter 27

Laura couldn't remember much about the accident at first but gradually, as she lay there recovering in hospital, going over and over the events in her mind, she began to formulate a clear picture of what had happened. She remembered walking the damp streets dazed and confused; she remembered the young couple stopping and offering her help; she remembered Lewis' black Audi screeching to a halt alongside them and she could almost feel the pressure on her arm as he forced her down into the car. She winced at the thought of it. She remembered the smeared windscreen as her screams filled the car and each time she closed her eyes, she could see the grey stone wall of the bridge looming towards her. And it always finished the same way – an explosion of noise wrapped in whirling chaos – and then total darkness.

Laura was doing well. She was making a good recovery. She had been moved out of Intensive Care within twenty-four hours and she was in a small side ward with five other beds. Numerous 'get well' cards were crammed onto a small bedside cabinet, most of them from her pupils at school. She was breathing freely and the swelling to her face had gone down, leaving a mass of bruises that were already turning brownish-yellow at the edges. Her parents were in and out constantly, comforting and reassuring and often just sitting for hours in complete silence. Laura had always found it difficult to talk to her parents and they were still not fully aware of the circumstances that had led to the accident. Matt had met Laura's parents on more than one occasion. At first, he had struggled to explain his relationship to Laura, describing himself as a 'close friend'. It had seemed to satisfy them. They weren't really that interested – particularly when they realised that he hadn't been there on the night of the crash.

Laura had taken the news of Lewis' death badly. They had told her as soon as she was moved out of Intensive Care and she had broken down and wept uncontrollably until the sedation kicked in and she had slept heavily. After that, she didn't mention him but in the days that followed she was filled with guilt. If only she had stood firm and refused to go to Dougie's party; if only she hadn't confronted Lewis in the kitchen; if she hadn't stormed out into the night . . .

Was the crash really her fault? Would she have to live the rest of her life carrying the burden of Lewis' death?

Meg popped in to see her regularly and Dina had already turned up twice, complete with new girlfriend – a smartly dressed forty-something with tightly cropped hair, who Laura later learned was a Deputy Head from a neighbouring school.

And then there was Matt. She was so pleased to see him that first time she regained consciousness that she just cried and cried. He joined in, not too sure exactly why he was crying but grateful to be included in her grief. She wouldn't talk much, at first, realising that she had hurt him, had let him down badly, but gradually she relaxed and conversation became easier. By Thursday evening she had even begun to smile again.

'I don't know why you're here,' she said, easing herself up into a sitting position. 'Not after the way I treated you.'

'I don't know why I'm here either,' he admitted. 'I was afraid you wouldn't want to see me. And I hate hospitals! They're not healthy places at all!'

Laura did her best to smile.

'I've made such a mess of my life, Matt. And Lewis – I feel so guilty.'

Matt took hold of her hand and held it gently. 'It wasn't your fault, Laura. You weren't to blame. If it hadn't been you in the car it would have been someone else. That's what Lewis was like.'

'I should have seen through him, Matt. I should have realised what he was like. I was running away from him and he dragged me into the car . . .'

'I know what happened,' interrupted Matt. 'Meg's told me everything. But you haven't made a mess of your life, Laura. You can't think like that. You'll come through this and you'll be stronger for it. You can get back to work and make a career for yourself, which is more than I can do.'

'I'm not going back to work, Matt. I'm going to move away. I can't stay round here. I won't be able to forget.'

The words cut into Matt like a knife. He couldn't speak for a moment and then he said, stutteringly, 'Where will you go?'

'I don't know yet. Wherever there's a teaching job. They're crying out for teachers in some areas.'

'Are you sure that's what you want?' said Matt. 'It's only been a few days. Perhaps if you give it time?'

'I've made my mind up,' said Laura. 'I don't need to give it time. As soon as I feel up to it I'm going to hand in my resignation at St Gregory's. I'll look for something else from the beginning of January. New year, new start and all that.'

Matt was silent for a few moments, and then, as if remembering he said, 'I'm leaving, too.

I've sold the house.'

'I know,' said Laura. 'Meg told me. What are you going to do?'

'I'm going back to Whitby. I leave in a fortnight. I've got a flat but I haven't got a job yet. I can live on what I've made from the house until I find something. It's not a lot but it will see me through.'

'Why did you decide to move?' asked Laura. She felt she knew the answer but she wanted to hear it from Matt.

'I was getting stale,' lied Matt. 'Going nowhere. A bit like you, really – I just want a new start.'

It was Laura's turn to fall silent. They sat there, the two of them, staring down at the white bedcover. Eventually, Laura raised her eyes and said, 'Can we keep in touch, Matt?'

'Of course we'll keep in touch,' he said. 'I'll come and see you. When you've got your new job, I mean.'

'I don't suppose . . .' began Laura, and she paused and took a deep breath.

'What?' said Matt. 'You don't suppose what?'

'I don't suppose there are many teaching jobs going near Whitby?'

He stared at her for what seemed like an eternity, and then his face broke into a smile.

'Well,' he said, leaning forward and

squeezing her hand tighter, 'you've got somewhere to stay while you look for one, haven't you?'

Book Club Questions for Discussion

'Mediocrity is the curse of the modern world'. The book starts with this statement, which reminds Matt of his own tedious, routine existence. Yet his job and, to an extent, his social life, are no different to the way in which many people live their own lives. How does the fact that Matt is not in a relationship impact on his life?

Routine plays a huge part in most of our lives, necessity often dominating the way we live. Discuss Matt's routine and contrast it with your own. Discuss both similarities and differences.

What was Matt's first impression of Laura? Subsequently, why do you think Laura agreed to go out with Matt?

The past seems an ever present place for Matt. He harks back to his childhood in Whitby, to his university years, to his failed relationship with Lydia. Discuss the way in which the past has shaped Matt's character.

Laura comes across as a rather confused character – someone who is at a crossroads in her life. In your opinion, what does Laura really want from life?

The sub-plot involving Linton weaves in and out of the main plot. Linton's youthful problems and his predicaments contrast with Matt's situation, yet their lives touch. Discuss further the relevance of the sub-plot.

What is your impression of Beano? Is he really just an uncouth oaf? How do you think Matt views Beano? Why does he remain friends with him? (Beano was the first person Matt turned to when he was really down.)

Discuss Laura's relationship with Lewis. Why was she so attracted to Lewis and why did she not finish the relationship as she discovered what he was really like?

Discuss the significance of the contrasting settings in the story – Didsbury and Whitby.

Matt's life seems to be dogged by missed opportunity, both in Didsbury and in Whitby. Discuss.

Do you think Matt made the right decision to sell up in Didsbury and return to Whitby? What do you think the future holds for Matt and Laura?

Missing Link

Elizabeth Kay

Spliff laughed softly. "Perhaps outright murder is the only thing we'll stop at on Missing Link. Because just when you all think it can't get any worse, it does . . ."

Jessica Pierce is a guest on the investigative chatshow *Missing Link*. The hugely popular programme is hosted by Spliff, a quick-thinking media-savvy presenter.
The show features two guests; they will never have met before. But a "heaven or hell" link between them is revealed – either something wonderful, such as a long-lost relative, or something appalling, like a false identity.
Spliff violently disapproves of the way television has been dumbed down and he decides to make a programme which will be so shocking that the series will be taken off the air, questions will be asked, and maybe television will be the better for it.
So when Spliff decides to go out with a bang, who will he take with him? . . .

"*Missing Link* teases you, tempts you to think you're as smart as the programme makers who manipulate, backbite and play out cut-throat rivalries behind the scenes. Just when you think you've got its measure—as tart satire on mass entertainment, as comedy of manners, even as romance—it opens a trapdoor on dizzying questions of science and morality. Like its enigmatic and dark-edged romantic lead, Elizabeth Kay's prescient novel layers its witty and intricate mind games with a heartfelt indignation, and even a hint of human vulnerability."
Philip Gross, Author

"**A skilled and ingenious piece of work**"
Fay Weldon, Author

ISBN 978-1-905637-88-1 £6.99

A Death in the Family

Caroline Dunford

I briefly considered the option of swooning in a ladylike manner, but I was denied this by virtue of position: I was a maid; and by natural inclination: I have never known how to swoon. Instead I did what I believe most females of sensibility would have done finding themselves alone with a murdered corpse. I screamed exceedingly loudly, quite in the common manner, and pelted out of the room . . .

In December 1909 the Reverend Joshia Martins expires in a dish of mutton and onions leaving his family on the brink of destitution. Joshia's daughter, Euphemia, takes it upon herself to provide for her mother and little brother by entering service. She's young, fit, intelligent, a little naive and assumes the life of a maid won't be too demanding. However, on her first day at the unhappy home of Sir Stapleford she discovers a murdered body.

Euphemia's innate sense of justice has her prying where no servant should look and uncovering some of the darker secrets of the Stapleford family. All she has to defend herself with is her quick wits, sense of humour and the ultimate weapon of all virtuous young women, her scream.

Euphemia tells the tale in a light-hearted way, writing in a style akin to a cross between Jane Austen and Agatha Christie.

'A sparkling and witty crime debut with a female protagonist to challenge Miss Marple.'
Lin Anderson, Award winning Scottish crime author and screen writer

ISBN 978-1-905637-90-4   £6.99

PUBLISHING

A Measure of the Soul

Stephanie Baudet

*The phone rang. Sighing, she went
back into the hall and picked it up,
lifting the earpiece to her ear.*

'Hello?'

*'I see they didn't find him,' said a voice.
'You obviously have him well hidden.'*

Harriet gasped. 'Who is this?' [. . .]

*'Did you really think you could hide
a deserter? How naïve you are,
Miss Baker.'*

For Harriet Baker, looking after her ailing father is a distressing burden but after his death she is faced with more problems and must cope alone.

It is 1918, the final year of the Great War, and when her brother, Alex, goes missing while on compassionate leave, she fears he will be shot for desertion.

Harriet hides him while the police search the house, never sure just how he will react in his shell-shocked state, and when he is seen by others, she is forced to yield to blackmail and can confide in no-one, not even her best friend, Gwen...

ISBN 978-1-905637-89-8   £6.99

Spectacles

Pippa Goodhart

For days after that it was as if I'd died and gone to Heaven. The world was so full of beauty! . . . Seeing the world so clearly felt like falling in love all over again . . .

When her domineering Mother dies, Iris is shocked by what she finds when clearing out her flat. It turns out that Iris is illegitimate. So she isn't the person she'd thought she was. Perhaps she can reinvent herself now?

When Iris acquires a pair of spectacles, she gains a renewed focus on life. She gives us her vision of the world around her, a clear, sometimes almost painfully comic view of people, places and the Meaning of Life! This complicated old woman shares some episodes from her life that move from gentle humour and pure farce to moments of tragedy and deep despair. Iris is always full of surprises, and she leaves the biggest surprise till the end of the novel, when she shocks the reader with the most poignant, eye-opening revelation of all.

Throughout this potpourri of a novel, Goodhart writes with humour and pathos as we follow this wonderful old woman [...] on an emotional journey.
Alan Wright, Author, nominated for *Debut Dagger* Award

A moving story of life, death and all the questions in between.
Louise Heyden, Librarian

ISBN 978-1-905637-86-7 £6.99

PRINT
PUBLISHING